The Journals
of An
Invisible
Man

1

Hello Reader, you have my journal, as you are the chosen one that the journal is meant for. Now this may seem a strange way to start a book, but then again this is not a book, but the writings of me, the Invisible Man.

Why Invisible? No, not like H. G. Wells invisible, like the Big Issue Seller or Homeless asleep on the streets. Millions pass by never seeing them.

Sat at Exeter Cathedral I watch as the man in a big red jacket selling the Big Issue is passed by, almost everyone without the slightest acknowledgement of his existence. I do not blame the people with their busy lives or even waste time to pontificate about our criminal government who in another time would of been hung for war crimes for the way in which they presently treat the people on the poverty line, promoting cruel indifferences as a harsh bitter 'Thatcherism' of "I'm alright Jack" attitude returns. I see the lonely and the poor. I see the weak and afraid. I see many disappear in the harsh cold night buried in pauper's graves; one less statistic on the government's fact sheets.

Three thousand heart attacks a week, eight hundred and eighty-nine people every day diagnosed with cancer, and yet the government feels it is up to us, we the people through our charitable nature should help, and thanks to you all, we do. Blindly, caring, remembering the visible and fighting to carry on with their lives trying to make sense of the pain.

So I sit here invisible, alone. Nobody special, no affiliations, just me, another Invisible Man. Sat here after a night in a casino in London I drove overnight down the M4 to the M5 to see sunrise in Exeter. A pretty city in Devon, boring, but pretty. I see the Big Issue Seller and give him a tenner from my winnings on the blackjack table. It had been a good night and I had managed to park the car in an empty, no yellow line street, and buy a ticket to New York. There is much going on and I am needed on the streets over the pond. The people there seem lost. The voice of the people, the press, lost years ago, now used as a tool to blind the vulnerable with lies and twisted facts to manipulate the wrong decisions being made as necessary.

Yes, as an Englishman we find the Americans strange, as they think we are eccentric, but I love them, I really do, as when you go there and spend time with them on mass they are a great people. They are also the most misrepresented humans in the world. Like many, like you my reader, I have heard stories and let myself generalise so often that even I have lost sight of the individual.

I remember that a Mosque was to be built near the ground zero site. I was overjoyed for once something to symbolise that 9/11, from a tragedy waiting to happen, yet in this one courageous action we would see good prevail over evil. Sadly, world press reports that the Americans were up in arms and threatening to blow it up. In reality one pastor with a congregation of less than one hundred and twenty, consisting of inbred loons, were actually responsible for this outcry. America, land of the free, over three hundred and twenty million people misrepresented in the press due to the voice of one, who pretends to be a man of God, one out of three million plus is given the platform to ignite wars so that the big businesses that own the manufacturing arms of ammunitions can make billions off the misery that follows, and in America waking that day, most knew nothing of the hatred they were labeled with.

So I am off to New York on a flight from Exeter via Amsterdam to help stop another catastrophe from happening. At least I will try. Once more drifting through the streets of New York invisible, unseen and able to move in and out of all circles with a few suits and social skills, I shall maneuver myself to make the man heard. Who is the man? Who am I? Well read on my friend as together we travel overseas and see the world as only the truly invisible man can.

I look at my watch and stand to make a move to the airport. As I look and smile at the seagull sat on the statues head I see a young college girl slip and fall. I move towards to help only to see a young boy help her up and smile. She has grazed her knee and the young man removes a clean handkerchief from his pocket and offers it to her. She dabs her bleeding knee and laughs at how silly she was to trip. The young man holds her bag patiently whilst the young girl composes herself. It is in moments like these I see the world has a chance. A young mind untainted, still pure of heart and sees the people around, all visible.

I look at the Big Issue Seller who smiles back at me. For a moment he sees me and I see him. We exchange the most basic of human needs. The desire to be noticed. He notices me hoping I will acknowledge him letting him know that I noticed him too. I smile once again at the Big Issue Seller and walk towards him. As we pass he remarks, "Nice to see, eh?"

"Yes", I reply, "I think today is going to be a good day".

"I agree" comes his reply, and after a smile he looks at me to say, "Today I woke up, therefore it is a good day". I smiled and thought on his remark and realised I had seen something truly wonderful with someone truly wise, and yet to most of the people rushing past the cathedral it was invisible.

Wishing him well I walk off to gather my stuff to go to the airport, my plane leaves in seven hours. I pass a coffee shop and look to my watch and decide to have a nice hot sweet latte. Sat drinking I again thought of all that had happened only moments ago. Thinking on what the Big Issue Seller said I realised that there was a man who has lived in the centre of a thousand stories, now at the lower side of society, like so many on the poverty line, but even though invisible to many, who feel that they are superior, they will never know the true wisdom as seen through his eyes.

Refreshed and with my bags I walk into the high street and off towards Exeter Central Train Station to see a beautiful young girl help an elderly old man into a breakfast bar she works in. I hold the door for them and the old man smiles at me and with an incorrigible grin laughs as he says, " Not trying to move in my date are you young man?" We all laugh and it seems the young lady, called Isobel, owns Brody's, the breakfast restaurant, and saw the old man and offered him a free meal. I watch as she attentively walks him to a table and hear her offer full breakfast and endless tea. The old boy has the biggest smile on his face that one can ever hope to see in a lifetime.

I see Isobel look back over her shoulder at me watching, and smile. Our moment of connection broken, as the door to the cafe closes and I find myself alone on the street and walk on.

2

Thank you Exeter, as an Invisible I often see human nature I wish for still alive and well and my faith in our ability to rise above the wrongs of this world. Straight ahead the station.

Exeter Airport and for small city it is as busy as Heathrow. I pass a policeman that seems to be watching all that happens yet never notices me. He is watching a young Indian family, whose little girl aged 6, is running round in circles and laughing. I smile at the sight; the policeman surveys without emotion. He has put on his uniform, hung up all his identity as a human being and is now in 'supercop' mode. I see him watching like he is in stealth mode. To him this innocent Indian mother and father with six-year-old daughter could be the terrorists he has been reading about. Why only yesterday Brussels was bombed following on from the Paris tragic events, this idiot in a uniform looks at the little girls my little pony backpack as a possible suicide bomb. I watch him stiffen in fear as the little girl reaches into the backpack. 'Supercop' is ready, hand held tight on his walkie talkie ready to rush her, save the day, then low and behold, the little terrorist pulls out a my little pony toy horse. Who would of thought it?

I watch this racist buffoon relax and walk on to another part of the departure lounge as a man in a turban has caught his eye and has his unbridled attention. He is so transfixed that I reach into my carry on and make out I have pulled out a gun and pretend to shoot him. Nobody sees me, all eyes are on the Turban, no wait, a colleague has joined him and someone else has caught his eye.... a young black girl. Now the two policemen are confused whom to watch, the Turban, possible terrorist or the Black girl, possible drug smuggling mule? I see them look to each other and call in on their walkie-talkies that they have a situation. Just as our two 'supercops' explain what the dilemma is, two farmers dressed in security uniforms arrive and all agree how to best team up and follow.

Hold on, hold on reader! What is this? The black girl acknowledges the Turban. Seems they know each other. She is running over to the Turban. In the confusion the two policemen and farmers dressed in security uniforms bump into each other watching each of their suspects, but all is too late, the black girl is warmly greeted by the Turban. They hug and exchange huge smiles and compliment each other. I watch as they laugh oblivious to the attention their colour and headgear had caused. I continue to watch as they laugh and ask each other what they are doing at the airport and where they are each going? Seems they are on the same flight and used to go to school together.

The original 'supercop' is walking away as the little Indian girl taps him on the leg. He stops and looks down and smiles as the little girl shows him her pony.

"This is Starlight."

The policeman crouches down and smiles, "Hello Starlight" he says and I see the man inside the uniform. I walk on and think the morning's briefing the policeman received at the start of duty leave his mind, all the negativity and fear disperse, and the human being returns.

I walk past the newspaper stand to see headlines that UK on high terrorist alert, again. It seems that as long as we tell the people to fear things we should welcome, in that I mean tolerance for freedom of speech, listen and ignore or join a real debate, then we will always be on terrorist alert. In fact when have we not been on terrorist alert?

As I pass through customs I see the black girl and guy in turban being passed through extra security. Alongside them, an irate white businessman. The young girl and boy chat on oblivious to the casual racism and carry on as f all matter of fact. I am suddenly ushered through and can hear the irate businessman complaining as it is obvious he is not a terrorist, to which the beautiful boy in the turban replies, "Me too. But happy they search everyone at random". The young man in the turban looks at the security guard who hangs his head in shame and cannot look him in the eye as too embarrassed.

"Sorry to of kept you sir", says the security guard to the man in Turban, "and you too miss" to the black girl. "Please both of you have a nice flight."

The young couple smiles and walk off engrossed in their conversation, oblivious of everything around them. The young black girl rushes back as she forgot her bag in the commotion.

I then hear in a direct tone the security guard say to the businessman, "Now sir, anymore from you and it will be a full strip search." The security guard looks at the black girl as if to say sorry just doing as I was told and she graciously smiles and winks, "No worries, and keep up the good work", looking at the businessman still fuming. I watch as she chases after the man in the Turban calling after him. "Samir, wait up", Samir turns and you can see he is smitten and I look at the security guard watch and sigh as he oodles the pretty black girls bum and realise she was visible all the time. "Come on Suzie, don't want to miss the plane" shouts

Samir and I smile. Off they walk giggling to the departure lounge and I overhear them again talk about things since leaving Exeter University two months ago. Both having wonderful plans for a life full of fun and adventure in New York, both have jobs and both staying in St Marks. What a coincidence.

Coincidence is rare and to have so many coincidences often men's greater forces at work. No I am not religious and not some Star Wars fanatic preaching the force, but often things come together as they are destined to do so.

Finally we are boarding the plane. I see in business class the businessman walking strangely, agitated and pulling his shorts from his backside as if he had been..... yes he had.

I board the plane and as I sit I see I am sat next to Samir. He graciously smiles and moves for me to sit next to him, but I stop and survey the plane to see Suzie sat with the Indian family.

"One second", I say to Samir. I make out I have mislaid my wallet and walk to the flight attendant, who is a stunning looking woman, and whisper in her ear. Her name is Marjorie, obviously I realised this from her nametag, as we Invisible People have not got super powers that can deduct people's names from whispering in their ear. Marjorie looks to the Indian family and smiles and motions for me to wait one moment. I notice Samir look at me confused, and he seems tired of being sidelined due to his look, and feels again racially directed at him due to his Turban by me. He looks forlorn and upset.

As I see Marjorie in the other aisle I walk back to Samir and pick up my carry on. Samir looks at me as if he is truly hurt. I turn to Samir.

"Please note this is nothing personal, but felt that you would rather sit with someone else than me."

Samir looks confused and then sees Marjorie walking Suzie down the aisle towards us. I move on and squeeze past them. I look back to see Samir's face beam with joy and excitement and look at me as if to say sorry, but his excitement to sit next to Suzie soon engulfs his apology and as she looks back I have already disappeared and taking my seat with the Indian family.

3 I am able to see from my advantage point the two friends light up as Suzie thanks Marjorie and sits next to Samir. I slink out of view and smile. I knew that within seconds they would be giggling and in full conversation where they left off, and yes I could hear they were. I am bought back to earth as sat on aisle seat next to Indian family the little girl pushes her little toy pony in my face. Next to me is the businessman who had been ejected from business class as his upgrade had been turned down. He looks at the Indian family and gives them a look of displeasure. The little girl looks at me and smiles and I smile back.

"Would that be Starlight?", I ask.

The little girl rushes to her father squealing with delight.

"Daddy, Daddy, that man knows Starlight".

Her father smiles to me, and the plane starts to taxi to the runway. I start to relax and think about New York the mission and….. oh yes coincidence. Remember I talked of coincidence; well sometimes it needs a little help. Samir and Suzie were in full flight of catch up stories and it had only been a couple of months apart.

The plane is packed and we have not even managed to get to the runway before the businessman has started complaining. This was going to be a long flight I thought. Then suddenly we race forward and we are off the ground hurtling into the air and signs are removed saying keep your seat belts on. A few seconds later Marjorie crouches next to me and whispers in my ear.

"There is a seat in first class you can have", she whispers.

I look to the little Indian girl and then at the businessman scowling at her across me mumbling, twitching and moving from the full cavity search from earlier and ask Marjorie, "Would you do me one last favour?"

Marjorie looks at me and smiles. The sort of smile that ends up in a compromising position about one mile in the air. I whisper in her ear and she looks back at me slightly confused, but then gives me a sly kiss on the cheek.

Standing Marjorie leans over me and taps the businessman on the shoulder.
" Excuse me sir?"

"This is hopeless love, this seat is awful," he snaps.

"Would you follow me as we are going to offer you a first class seat", you could hear the words almost stick in Marjorie's throat.

The businessman suddenly looks excited then apologetic, then embarrassed, as he feels guilty, all in the split of a second.

"Are you sure?" he asks.

"Go my friend, enjoy the flight" I say to him and stand to let him pass. As he rises he stops to feel he should offer me the seat and I smile and let him pass. Graciously he accepts and whilst looking guilty and full of remorse he follows Marjorie in to the first class seating. As he is about to pass into first class the businessman looks back to me as I take my seat. Yet I do detect a hint of excitement in the gleam of his eye.

"Watch out for Starlight," he says and exits as Marjorie looks back at me as if she is going to give me the best seeing to since the beginning of time.

Funny thing was all this happened and I was completely invisible to all, except Marjorie. Oh Marjorie, what a fantastic woman…. sorry reader, but sometimes you meet a woman so splendid she takes your breath away with her smile, this was Marjorie.

Oh and of course the little Indian girl and Starlight, they can see me, in fact at least two hours of the flight whilst a very tired mummy and daddy sleep Starlight and Surabhi, my little new best friend watched My Little Pony cartoons until she fell asleep and Marjorie helped settle her in her seat out for the count. The little girl's father tired looked at me to speak, but I just said what a joy Surabhi was and he smiled and fell back to sleep himself.

We are now three hours into the flight and I need the little boys room. My dear reader this is a journal not a kiss and tell gratuitous novel! I needed to stretch my legs and relieve all the drinks I had drunk whilst watching My Little Pony.

I walk to where the toilets are next to the air hostesses station and as I write this journal reader I wish it was at this moment Marjorie dragged me into the cubicle and made mad passionate love to me, but no, I was stood waiting after a portly gentleman, sadly drunk and had not left the cubicle as he found it. I see Marjorie and her colleague notice and grab a cleaning bucket discreetly, which I take from her and enter the cubicle. It was a mess, but not too bad and moments later when I had finished I exited and handed back the cleaning bucket, smiled and walked back to my seat; turning slightly to notice both Marjorie and her colleague look in to see how clean I had left it.

I looked over at Suzie and Samir, still in full flight, talking as ferociously as before. I cannot help thinking they did so much in two months to discuss or were so oblivious to how much in love they were neither wanted to stop.

I look back at Marjorie and she motions for me to join her at the station. I walk back and looking at this complete vision in a uniform I try to stay cool, but trip over Starlight and after picking up Surabhi's toy pony and placing it gently in her arms I look up to see Marjorie and her colleague smiling laughing.

Again another dazzling smile from Marjorie and I walk to the attendants' station.

"We wish all our passenger's were like you," said Marjorie and introduced me to Giselle her colleague.

"Giselle and I share a flat in New York, and thought if you ever are in our neighbourhood you are more than welcome, here is my address and number."

I graciously thank them and walk back to my seat knowing they are checking my bum out. Now I am not a piece of meat ladies, but I do like the compliment.

As I return to the seat Starlight is again on the floor as well as Mother's blanket. I pick up both and carefully place them back as Surabhi's father wakes and smiles at me. I start to sit in my chair and see Suzi look oblivious to Samir at her purse for cash and she has none. She closes the purse and returns to chat. I look to see Marjorie chatting to a passenger, but Giselle has her eye on me. I call Giselle over and whisper in her ear. Giselle looks at me, and laughs as if to say are you sure, then as I nod she walks the long way round back to pass Suzi.

I watch as Giselle whispers in Suzi's ear and Suzi looks at her as if to say, 'are you sure?' I smile and after a few seconds Giselle returns with a bottle of Prosecco and two champagne flutes. Samir looks as if to say he shouldn't and then looks at Suzi to say why not. They are amazed to hear they were in the two seats that were in the raffle for the flights free drink draw. I sit back and relax as we start to near our destination, New York. Seems I am not as invisible as I thought and my mind returns to my mission.

Now reader I have written the word 'mission' as stated before, I am a happy nobody, invisible to most and happy to observe and help where I can those that may need a hand sometimes; and yes Samir has just kissed Suzie, who'd of seen that coming? Bubbles, the joy of being in love.

I may laugh at myself sometimes as I am no 00 agent, I may smile and sometimes I play act being one, but when I catch my reflection in the mirror or a shop window I suddenly stop, become self-conscious wondering how long I had been acting the fool and had anyone seen?

I once stopped in Bond Street on the way to meet a friend at BAFTA and behind me a tall beautiful Russian girl had been watching. I smiled at her and she walked over to me like in a spy thriller movie speaking in a soft, sexy broken English voice, "Hello, want to play with me?"

I am afraid to say I smiled back awkwardly and embarrassed as wondered what I was doing to provoke the offer.

She continued, " No seriously, I would love to roll play with you. I find you very sexy. I would halve my normal fee and do you for £400."

Thinking Russian call girls were more expensive than imagined I made my excuses and wished her well. As I walked to BAFTA I remember she did not take my rejection to her offer well and shout after me, "Faggot, bum boy!"

A man in a bowler hat thought she was shouting at him and turned to see if there was anyone else she was shouting at, but I had disappeared, become invisible again. I do hope the chap in the bowler hat got the discount though.

The Captain speaks over the planes intercom system to announce that we are due to land in Newark, New York. I look round to see I had been daydreaming and was actually sat with different people on the second plane. I had a connecting flight in Amsterdam and I remember very little as obviously more tired than I had realised. This is something you may need to note reader, I often blackout. I always rise in the morning with an erection. Possibly more information than necessary I hear you think, but in this case relevant as I wake and find an attractive girl laying on the three seats in the aisle next to me and her head in my lap. Yes, you guessed, well thanks for keeping up, as sadly I was too. I looked down and was in a little discomfort, as my new friend was lying on the one spot that needed adjusting.

I carefully eased her head up, she was spark out. Manage to release the tension and then carefully let her head down gently again. Sadly, my unruly friend in my trousers new position and rigidness had made the pillow effect less comfortable and my new friend, whom I cannot ever remember wakes and looks at me. First she smiles, then shock and then sits bolt upright, confused and in shock and anger. So my blackout on this journey means that I too have no answer to what is what.

"What the Feck do you think you are doing?" She was Irish Jewish, a potent combination. Realising she was face down in my crotch she rose quickly, blood rushing to her head, looking at me as if I had drugged her or something, looks around to see where she is, and stands as a blanket placed over her falls down and reveals she has her trousers undone.

"Help! Help!", she cries, and manages to catch the attention of everyone on the plane, except on old guy who was asleep and his hearing aid had fallen out.

Suddenly, to my amazement, the wonderful Marjorie is there by my side. I look at her confused and Marjorie winks at me.

"This guy molested me!" she cries. Yes, it got worse, and I still have not a clue. Suddenly I am visible, I looked confused; I was confused. I have no recollection of how I got there, let alone the girl, but all I knew was Marjorie was there.

"Miss, please Miss, calm yourself", and the girl looks to see everyone staring at her and not me. Marjorie continues to explain, and I was truly grateful as this was as much news to me as it was the girl, that she had been more than slightly drunk and was going to be ejected, but this gentleman, me, offered to help, held countless sick bags she used, and looked after you until about an hour ago as we were a little short staffed. Turns out I had been a real gent. The girl looked at me and then at the whole plane watching as she remembered the flight's events. Looking back at me she seemed crest fallen.

Marjorie explained that she and Giselle undid her trousers as she was bloated.

"I am so sorry, I had no idea", the girl said. I returned a smile to say no worries and then half relieved, more wishing to stay invisible, but soon became visible as she launched into a loud statement, shouting I suppose, to all still watching,

"It's OK, my mistake. Seems this guy is not a pervert".

The old guy with his hearing aid looks up from his slumber and at me.

"Blimey, mate, even I heard that!", he remarks and closes his eyes again.

Then a sudden rush of adrenaline courses through the girl's body and the enthusiasm for thinking of arriving and making things right takes hold of her new acquaintance, my hand. She squeals in delight. Then with adrenaline rushing through every vein of her body she looks to me to say that she wants to introduce me to her fiancée. It is at this moment that I realise she is standing, as she is such a cute little thing, no more than five foot tall. I smile and nod whilst looking at my over excited friend, acknowledging that I cannot wait, but deep inside longing to be invisible again.

As the taxi docks I again see my five-foot friend is obviously having trouble getting to the overhead locker. I stand and help as she stretches. She is a really pretty girl, shapely figure; we exchange smiles as I pass her her hand luggage. In no time at all we are shuffling down the aisle to the exit the plane. I see Giselle and Marjorie at the doorway and our eyes meet once more.

"Thanks for flying with me," she says mischievously.

"Best ride of my life," I reply and smile as I exit.

As I exited the plane part of me died. I could not believe I just said that. Come on reader was that not crass? Daft? Stupid? Or do you think I could of said worse? Have you?

Waiting for luggage I place my hand in my pocket and find Marjorie's card. I smile. I look back from where we came off the plane and thought that, who knows, may be one day I will see Marjorie again. But for now I was invisible again. Among the crowd. I pass Samir and Suzie still in full conversation, just as ferociously and full on as when they first met. I reflect on looking at them and wonder if they know just how perfect they are for each other. They do not notice me I am invisible again; mind you Suzie and Samir notice no one but themselves either. I hear a shrill voice cry out behind me, " Hey Mister wait for me!"

Yes it is my diminutive new friend. There she is dragging a huge case, the case was bigger than her. I think how she could go caravanning in that case. She stands below me and I find myself helping her with her case. She is bubbly and full of life talking at three hundred words a minute. A retired Marine home from duty reacts as if he just heard a machine gun going off and looks at me and smiles. He raises an eyebrow and walks on laughing. "Yes, Go ahead fella, have a laugh, she's not even with me, I don't even know her name" I cry after him, well think, as never say as she is still below me chatting. I look down at her and smile and think how pretty she is then am drawn to look over her head by a presence calling to me with her rapturous beauty. Marjorie walks past, sees me, smiles and motions to call her. I dumbly salute... yes I salute reader, I guess I still have the Marine in my head and seems in the moment I am actually unable to make an appropriate gesture. Marjorie just smiles back and exits with crew. Following behind is Giselle who also spots me and motions call us.

I am bought back in the room as I hear my diminutive friend say in loud stage whisper, " I am so glad you turned out not to be a pervert".

An elderly British woman misheard as she walked passed and gives me a look of disgust. Followed behind by the old man with the hearing aid who smiles at me and suddenly speaks to me,

21

"Don't worry she just misheard. Oh, the hearing aid, I don't need it, just use it to make myself invisible when she has something she needs to tell me," and with a wry smile he laughs and walks on. I hear the British Lady cry out "Wilbur, will you keep up?" and see the old boy follow and smile saying, " Sorry dear, what did you say?" I watch as the woman walks off in a huff and the old man looks back to me and smiles the biggest smile I think I have ever seen. I think letting someone know his secret gave him the most pleasure imaginable.

I was now in the customs area and in all the commotion realised I had not filled in the entry visa card and collect one to fill in. At least this gives me an excuse to say goodbye early to my little friend. As I watch her dragging a home for a Hobbit behind her I again think what a nice bum and good things do come in small packages. Oi! Come on reader that was not a euphemism…. really, but then again….

I look at the visa form and it says where you will be staying. I suddenly realise I bought flight only no hotel and have no address, then it dawns on me no address, no entry. I see Marjorie waft through customs and again she looks back to catch my eye, not that I have a glass eye and threw it at her reader, but every time I am in need Marjorie is there. Who needs St Christopher when you have the Divine Marjorie of the skies.

I stand in the non-US Citizen line and fill in Marjorie's address. My small scattergun chatterer is an American and is in the other queue. Soon I am at the desk.

I am asked to place my finger into a scanner and without thinking make a joke I could of regretted,

"Just for your information I am left handed, this is my trigger finger."

Rule of thumb, no pun intended, never joke with a five-foot, moustache, custom official from the US. They all have humour removed at birth. In fact in the exam to become a US Custom guard they are taken into a room screening Robin Williams Live and if they laugh, they're out.

But, my generous nature and will to help others comes to my rescue in two forms. Firstly, the customs guy has a crush on Marjorie and looks at me with a disdained look.

"OK Buddy, so you're a friend of Marjorie...."

Then he looks up and second sad piece of fate. The bigot in the customs uniform spots Samir in his turban. Suddenly the customs area is on high alert. It was both comical and sickening to see. The hysteria and fear in America, Land of the Brave etc etc etc, fear whipped up placing the well being of good people from America abroad at risk, fuelling stories that all Americans are a degenerate race that hate all except themselves.

"OK Buddy, move on", he says and then pulls out his walkie-talkie. "Tony we have a possible bogey in the hall, repeat possible bogey in the hall, do you copy, Over?"

At last I am invisible again and realise my mission here is even more urgent than I had thought. I walk into New York as an Invisible Man.......

"Hey, Mister? Over here!", a shrill voice cries out and immediately from her low vantage point the short travelling phenomenon has spotted me.

I smile as she rushes towards me and then escorts me to meet her fiancée; a six foot seven giant. Lots is racing through my mind wondering........

Well reader, I am sure you can guess thoughts going through my mind, all the comical situations running through my head. I for the first time notice she has a flat head and... I digress.

As I walk to meet the man mountain, an outstanding athlete figure of a man, my tiny friend is once again babbling at a hundred miles an hour. I am bought back into the room, figuratively speaking, as she clearly says, " So I was telling Randy how I awoke with my head in your lap and my trousers undone, of course I jumped to the wrong conclusion, and in fact you were my hero, my knight in shinning armour, not a pervert"

I winced at the last remark as the old British Lady walked past and grinning laughing at me was the old man with the deaf aid. I motioned to him to say the fake hearing aid was out and he popped it in his ear as the woman shouted, "Come On Wilbur, keep up!"

"Sorry dear? What dear?" he replied laughing as he said it looking at me.

I look back to see Randy holding out his hand to say thank you and still has a look of confusion on his face. I shake his hand and see mine engulfed in his like a bus ticket would be in mine. Strange analogy true, but I was struggling to comprehend the wedding photo nightmare once these two tie the knot.

Randy is incredibly gracious and totally smitten with his love. He is the American Dream; he is mannered and educated, athletic and cultured, gracious and genuine in his caring for those around him. Bit of a long description, but want to emphasise this is how most Americans are, or look to be, and are not as portrayed in the rest of the world.

I say something like," No worries, got to dash, and wish you both all the happiness", and put on my Red Sox baseball cap.

"Randy, Randy, he's a fan!" she exclaims.

Not knowing what she was on about I politely smile and walk to the taxi area. Standing in the queue there is suddenly a flurry of paparazzi flash bulbs and turn to see who is coming. Thought may be it is David Beckham, the most visible man in the world, but no, it was Randy. The whole taxi queue rush over to take selfies and I find myself walk straight into a cab that would drive me into Manhattan.

I was at last Invisible again and could now start my mission.

I jump out of the cab at Ground Zero. An eerie place that should of become a beacon of hope, yet one cannot move away from the anger and pain that this site emanates. Those that visit touch the ground, the railings the monument and cry, some angrily, shout out loud anti-Muslim rhetoric, and how they vow to kill them all. I walk past unnoticed and see a Big Issue Seller calling out whilst city boys and girls, bankers and lawyer types walk past as if he did not exist. The Big Issue seller is invisible, yet spots me and I walk over to him.

I offered to buy him a coffee and his last paper so we sit in a nearby coffee house Dougal and I. Yes, Dougal is his name and he served nine years in Iraq and Middle East. I offered him a cup of Joe and some lunch. He never asked for more than he thought was correct and he restored my faith in the American people.

Dougal was a maths major and joined the army, as there were no jobs at the time, he was expecting to work in statistics somewhere in the States.

After six months basic training he was stationed in Erbil in the north, yes North of Iraq, he tells me how he spent most of his time not fighting the Taliban, but the powers the United Nations under American pressure had sanctioned to lead the new country regime from genocide on the Kurds.

"It was a 'complete clusterfuck' he said. " No one will ever know the real truth"

Since returning and seeing how badly his fellow countrymen were behaving he felt the need to change faith, to become a Muslim as a protest. He then started to laugh and when able to regain his composure told me that after two days of having to stop and pray all through the day, he gave up.

"I've got a lot of respect for those Muslims, that religion is hardcore!"

We laughed and he did astound me as he still read the Koran and said how he is humbled by its non-violence mantra. But that as with Americans claiming wrongly the right to bear arms out of context, the fanatics have misrepresented the Koran to use as a weapon of war.

I remember on the plane over watching a brilliant film Spotlight about pedophile priests and we talked of how the children most vulnerable were pressed into being abuse victims out of fear, as to not go along would be going against the Priest and going against the Priest was like going against God, for the Priest is the word of God. The religious fanatics in the Middle Earth are much the same.

This led me to see the word on the street about a ruthless politician who was stirring the masses, fuelling hatred in people to take their own guilt for their misgivings. By helping people look to others for the blame for their lives not be as great as they see in the movies. This evil man was blind siding a whole nation momentarily to his alter devices. A momentary lapse that could lead to another mistake this great country could not afford to make.

We discussed the parallel rise of this man and that of Adolf Hitler and that in fact his followers were quoted Hitler as if this bozo looking to be President had said it and they agreed with the hate filled rhetoric of a Nazi as if OK in todays day and age.

I was then completely lost as the discussion changed and my Big Issue Seller was an admirer of this politician and was becoming a fan. After all we had discussed he was easily swayed into agreeing with a monster, as he was not happy with the other options before him. I moved off the topic as did not want to compromise my mission.

We discussed Presidents and he was an old school JFK fan. He felt that the powers behind the throne were responsible for the death of JFK. There were no conspiracy theories they were just the truth. JFK did not want to go to war in Vietnam and big business did, so they shot him. And they did it openly in front of the world; they wanted to show the next incumbent just how powerful they were. Why the hell did we go back with no WMD's? Same reason.

"Hell even Bobby Kennedy was shot as he wanted to leave Nam," he went on to conclude.

I saw an opening. I asked if he had read JKF's book 'While England Slept'? He had not. I wished he had. I noticed a second hand bookshop across the road and asked him to wait for me that I would be back, but he did not want to wait so we walked together. He was a more complex character than I could of imagined. Luck had it there was a copy of the book, I bought it and gave it to him for which he was truly grateful. As we parted I wondered if we would ever meet again, but felt if we did not then I wish him well for he has seen things through his eyes that I cannot imagine.

Dear Reader, I do not give people's full names, and actually Dougal was not called Dougal at all, as I trust you to keep this journal safe and away from the powers that run our world as if this falls into their hands many lives would be at risk.

You see this journal is basic code of practice for all to become Invisible and yet make a difference. Within the journal are quotes from other Invisible Men and Women who shaped much of society without anyone knowing. They try to influence the true realisations or revelations of what was or is actually going on around us.

I have always loved quotes from the immortal Mark Twain. Who has had his words misquoted and bastardised, yet the sentiment remained true.

One quote I will always live by from him was as follows; and I probably misquote, as on his deathbed in essence he said, allegedly,

"My life was full of problems that did not exist."

4 The code of the Invisible is to face our difficulties and deal with them, as they are never as bad as we feared. In fact to try to remove fear for it is fear and the use of fear that drives all the wrong doing in this world. Fear led Hitler to power, Fear is being used today and my mission is to expose the hatred behind the fear to enable the good people to see what the future could hold. Einstein said, and again I probably misquote'

"Evil men exist because good men sit idle and watch."

Make sure that the good is heard on your street and that such evil does not raise its head on our watch.

Walking the streets late at night I see many of the Invisible people that inherit every city, town, village, in every country, the homeless.

I never watch comfortably as everybody watches the lights and sights and literally step over people as if they are not there. This was New York, fast moving, brassy and open 24/7, yet no time is given to those that fall below the poverty line.

Just think about it reader, you and me on the streets, 42nd street walking up to Times Square. I am sure like many you think the homeless are all drug users and alcoholics. I am not saying that they are not, many are, they have become this on the journey falling through the gap, I agree many have addictions, many have mental illnesses, but the majority are mums and dads, sons and daughters, some with kids to feed, and yet if you took time to stop and talk you would find even the loony tunes and drunks never ask for more than they need.

They are courteous and always gracious when treated well. I have walked empty streets, empty of love, of pity; I was once homeless, had fallen through the gap and really although I never blamed anyone else, a case could be made to say otherwise. I digress another time reader.

The temperature on the streets is exceedingly cold this March and it seems the rain had fallen for most of the day as everywhere looked as if a film crew had wet down the streets for effect. I felt the cold and gazed at the lights reflecting and shimmering in the tarmac of the road.

With my rucksack and small carry on bag I had left Dougal and was starting think about looking for a bed for the night. I found myself travelling to Queens and an old bar that I have been to many times before. The bar does not close until 4am and is always packed. For an invisible this is important, no one around you get seen; large crowds, who is going to notice just you?

I hail a cab and start to feel homesick. How I miss London. The black cabs know literally every street, the knowledge it is called, and no matter where you are going they know how to get there by the quickest route. In New York the driver may not even know where Queens is. Luckily I manage to hail a cab driven by Abdul. Yes good American name. We laughed on the way to Queens as he tells me he got off the plane from Iran twenty years ago and got a job driving a cab immediately. He had twenty years knowledge, he knew this city, he knew the bar and in no time Abdul had me heading towards the bars lights shinning in the wet road in the distance.

The bar was noisy, what do you expect in Queens, and in full swing. I enter and spot Joe the owner. Joe DiMaggio they call him as he looks very much like the famous baseball player that once was married to Marilyn Munroe. By the way reader Joe calls me Alfred and thinks I play cards in Vegas. I never told him my name or what I do, but somehow Joe thinks this is the case and who am I to correct him?

The reason I do not write my name reader is purely as there is no need to. I am nobody special, just another Invisible Man. Of course as you read on there are clues to my real identity, but that is the point of the journal; we all have a desire to be noticed, to be recognised, and reminded that we are somebody, but I enjoy the anonymity of being invisible. Read on and you will come to know me and of course what my mission is. To be honest and give one clue is my mission is one long connected series of missions that add up to a life lived.

"Alfredo my old friend," I hear as Joe walks up to me, " You need a room? Of course you need a room."

I smile and hug my old friend then without a word from me Joe spins round and shouts,

"Gino, an American champagne for Mr. Alfredo."

This is an old joke for which I am know in many places. The barman looks confused and then Joe points to a bottle in the fridge and laughs a hearty laugh. Hey presto, one coca cola, no ice; well even we invisible have a usual.

The joke stems from my many visits to the Cannes Film Festival in May each year. My friends at the Majestic remember me each year and serve me with great pride, and loud voices, so all can hear, "American Champagne."

In the bar all the American stars and filmmakers look round with pride as if to say that here in France they serve American champagne only to be deflated as the coke bottle is served up.

"You still seeing Isobel, such a nice girl?" Of course it is Joe and I am back in the room. Isobel was another girl that I met at the bar years ago and Joe always remembers her. I think he was a little in love with her himself, but then who wouldn't be. She was a stunning red head with a curvaceous figure; great girl full of life. I think that Joe remembers me because when he sees me he thinks of her.

"No, not since that night here sadly Joe," I reply and as I drink my coke Joe hands me the key to room 22.

Now room 22 has a significant meaning to it as this is where whilst Joe DiMaggio was married to Marilyn Munroe that JFK met her to secretly have sex, so legend has it, and another reason my friend is called Joe DiMaggio. All I remember from a drunken evening, well the evening with Isobel, oh and Joe's real name was Alfredo Mott, I think I said that night to him that tonight I would be Alfredo for you and then he told me how all of his eight wives cheated on him. I guess reader, Joe was not the greatest of lovers, but always a great

33

host. Well for now not saying more on Isobel as I am an Englishman and will decline saying I blacked out.

I sat in the crowded bar watching people laugh and cheer as the atmosphere was buzzing. I like this bar as it houses every denomination, every religion; every level of society was here living in close proximity of each other. All knew each other, all helping each other out. Before I arrived there had been a tearful moment as an Italian family, father was a regular, toasted the bar and one city lad called Dominic, who had raised over seven thousand dollars to take their terminally ill daughter to Disneyworld in Florida and to swim with dolphins. I found again my faith in the human spirit restored as well as my love and appreciation for this great people called Americans. It seems often as a unit, as one, together, all had stopped to take notice of what was happening around them. We often do not see the details as we are only looking out for ourselves, so wrapped up in our own worlds, as if we are all that is we do not see those around us struggling.

Then I look up at the corner of the bar to see a television with subtitled news screening. Reporting on a businessman running for President. Fuelling hatred and fear, looking for scapegoats for the people to rally behind him, he had maneuvered himself as front-runner for the Republican candidacy. We had seen his like before blaming the Jews in Germany, this was a crass, evil man who used his wealth to pick on the poor and exploit them. He built his fortune from ripping off those around him, but picking on everyone not pure white American, he had rallied support. Well not in New York. New York was the city of immigrants.

It would be a bad day for the world if this dangerous clown fooled a great nation into a world of misery, as he was a moron on world affairs thinking Pakistan was the capital of India, I kid you not, he has spent his campaign lying and deflecting any question by raising fear and bigotry and stirring up the bad in people to blame the weak for their own misgivings.

I remember another great American President once said, and he was for me the greatest, Abraham Lincoln said many things but one that came to mind was something like, ' You can fool most of the people some of the time, some of the people all of the time, but you cannot fool all of the people all of the time'. Anyway, this flop haired bozo is the greatest threat to world stability and the end of America as a trusted super power. In fact if he was elected Americans might as well throw away their passports, as they would not be safe outside their own country.

This dear reader is my mission. To ensure the majority of the people see so that those blinded by their desire to not look at themselves as to why they are not successful, do not manage to produce a result in the election that would ultimate place the world at risk.

I look at the television once again and see all the political pundits highlighting how the Republican businessman has created a hysteria around himself and his campaign. That he stirs up controversy and instills hatred and fear into those that are weak enough to listen, yet has absolutely nothing to say about how he is going to do anything. Nothing constructive at all. He is building walls to keep people out and blaming immigrants ten generations old as prostitutes, pimps, drug dealers or murderers, and yet his businesses have acted with more of these traits than any minority living in America.

He installs in all the God Loving Folk around the country in this economic hiatus to look at all non-white people in their community and fuels their hatred against any minority in order to hide their own flaws; but mainly his own inadequacies. He boosts about his prowess with the ladies and I laugh as without his money the bimbos and whores he attracts would not go anywhere near the creep. Yet he continues and I wonder are the people blind, can they be this unhappy to be this dumb. Come on America, he says he wants to make America great again, you already are, but I do say to you listen to him say that and prove it by throwing this evil piece of crap out.

Sorry Reader, got a little heated there, I am human after all and I am not going to sit by and watch another Hitler rise in the free world.

Hitler you think too strong? Well still the disillusioned and unintelligent flock to his rallies, chant racist rhetoric, and act with violence never seen before in an American political arena. Somehow he has cast aside his opponents, another sorry bunch of losers and scum bags who thought they had some divine right to be president due to their wealth and birthright, railroaded past them with his juggernaut of hatred and fear campaign leaving them behind as also ran.

But part of me looks around the bar and the world Joe has created. A world of beauty and horror side by side, working together, accepting each other without question. Joe has created Utopia where I watch the TV screen above these great people, and watch the KKK go unchallenged, standing side by side with this moron close to power, unchallenged by the pundits strong enough so that his integrity is never challenged as he flicks their questions aside with more nonsense. As there is no one willing to stand up then this is what we, the Invisible do, I cannot blame the people for allowing this monster of hate and stupidity rise; no stupidity is an unfair comment.

This is a man who calculates his every move, knowing he runs rings around an amateur media who have not the ability to make him accountable for anything he says or does, he calculates as once did a brilliant man in Germany in the 1930's who saw such an opportunity, who also captured a disillusioned nation before making it his slave. I look at the fool spouting what he knows the mass uneducated want to hear. Blaming Mexicans and Minorities, instead of the Jews, Yes this is me, in fear of history repeating itself. For this man is just a reincarnation of other evil men hidden behind clever words and violence. I ask you, could America be finding us a new Hitler?

Hitler again? I hear you say, but reader think. He blames the weak minorities and sets people against their fellow countrymen, hiding his own devious agenda. He advocates and supports violence and openly says he would support and defend, paying legal bills, anyone who beats up another who questions the slightest words he may spew forth. The brown shirts are now white, the caps white hoods, Klansmen fill the assemblies ready to hit a Jew, a Black person, a Muslim, a Student, a Veteran, or a child if it offers one word of dissent or questions their leader.

He holds rallies charged on hate and now the balance of power seriously in jeopardy as he offends Russia, Mexico, The UK, Europe, Asia and his own people that dare to ask him to justify his actions and words. Words that change as often as his underwear and in honesty do the same job; keep the shit from coming into view. As I said I am angry and again say I do not blame the people.

Look closely reader at who the man is, his family. His wife a pornstar model and his children go big game hunting shooting defenseless animals as if they are part of a superior race. The idiots call it sport, give the lion a gun, let him have the ability to shoot back at you, you cowards that would be more of a sport. I would be ashamed to have any one of his turgid offspring as any kind of relative of mine. The pedophile even says if his daughter was not his daughter he'd bang her, she's hot. So this, my beautiful American friends is what you think should be your leader?

Sorry Reader time for a break.

5 I remember walking the streets in Exeter as a Home Fundraiser trying to help charities, although also felt we were helping the Home Fundraisers Company get richer as they get 30% I think, anyway they try to help charities find funding and at least make awareness. I had this really interesting chat with this university student who wanted to be a career politician. Never lived a life outside of school, privileged and was looking forward to shaping how we live. Yes, he was going to shape how we live having never been in the real world himself. Just blindly following the words told to believe from those that ruled his world.

In America career Presidents are born as puppets of the corporations. Only now and again does a man of the people truly rise. Obama the last of that breed, now once again corporations rise to get their man or woman in the big chair. But this time the corporations have a spanner in the works. A self centred businessman who will say whatever the people want to hear and hope that no one is truly listening or remembers what he actually said. And many are deaf as they are tired of the career politicians. Can we blame a people ostracised from all that is done and left to pay as the corporations' blunders are allowed to manipulate change in their favour? Banks bought about the current economic climate, left the people to pay for their mistakes, yet not one of the guilty even faced a trial.

So back to my mission Reader. I am here to find a way to wake up a nation. I am the Invisible Man and in history past, men and women have fallen as they stood up and were shot. Today we are able to stand up and speak without anyone knowing we are there, a conscience of the people and our anonymity makes us more powerful than those that rise trying to dictate, for we are all flawed and if the evil has nothing to attack they have to justify. That is where a silent majority has the power to defeat. True evil happens because too many good men stand idly by and do nothing; remember?

Joe breaks my train of thought and I am back in the room.

" Alfredo, we are having a sign song, you me do it my way?"

I smile and walk to the mic he has already set up at the bar. As I walk to the bar I see a small collection of activists who are going to tomorrow's rally. I wink at one girl and she smiles back as the music painfully starts. I stand alongside my tone deaf friend Joe, whilst watching the television reports, silent unnoticed with pictures of my intended target, reading the subtitles of the scary statements and watching him grin as he half heartedly down plays his joy at the rise in violence coinciding with his rise in power. He says it is just the people speaking. He thinks that he will be a great leader, a leader of men, visit the capital of India and once in Pakistan confront and kill the terrorists. He would personally deal with terrorism direct himself. I laugh in disbelief and we are halfway through the song as Joe hugs me singing off key as if we are on the same page.

Reader, you have this journal as you are the intelligent ones. The readers, the informed and you have the vocabulary to inform those that are blinded to the dangers ahead with this man. For they have been brainwashed with fear, fear that things will not get

40

better for them unless they irradiate the bad people that have put them in hard times, he has given them scapegoats and they are happy to blame others rather than take the blame themselves.

Reader, please keep this journal safe for should the large corporations know of my, or any of my thousands of colleagues invisibility, then our world would be over. Not just we would be found and exterminated, but the freedom we all hold dear would be extinguished as well. Once I know you are ready to become part of the invisible army too then I will hand over the baton and reveal myself happily resigned to die if needed to stop us from destroying the world through destruction by stupidity.

There is an eerie buzz in New York. It is as if something is about to happen, but we have no idea what it is. Most of New Yorkers continue about their business as if everything is the same. I cannot blame them as with all the troubles reported daily in the world it is good to see everyone get on with their lives. The terror threats and scaremongering last for the length of the report and in seconds it is old news and we, the people, how we deal with life after this is what makes us who we are. To shut out the negative is imperative or find a scapegoat and once established we admonish all responsibility from ourselves.

But we have a silent presence that offers one even greater threat. We have the equilibrium of world peace estate; we have an underground movement taking the security we enjoy from under our feet. A movement where friends become our foes. A world where everybody is putting into place his or her own agendas, a time the consequential change that would place the globe into a diplomatic darkness. For one man has whipped up a storm offshore bring his own political Katrina into town tonight. Tonight could be the dawn of an era not seen since the dark days preceding World War II.

As I leave Joe I see he has all the books on JFK and see the titles 'Profiles in Courage', and small piece he wrote called 'Why England Slept'. The latter was just a college thesis JFK wrote on why England stood by as Hitler used the time to amasses armies to start what would become World War II. He criticised the UK for not acting sooner, but in fact England use diplomacy at first, not an American trait sadly, and in that time Hitler grew England allied with the neighbours to stand together in their hour of need to defend our freedom.

But the irony is one of America's most beloved presidents saw that coming up for on the way Hitler stirred the week nature of Germany's worst traits he would truly recognise that the threat was as relevant today as back in 1933-39. With Internet and mass media my target had done in six months what Hitler took to do in six years. This mission suddenly sank home once more. My mission as an invisible man took on a more urgent nature as I stood there in Joe's bar.

It is funny as social media is awash with news and videos of tonight and sides posting videos of both parties representatives saying their candidate is better than their opponent, and is funny as I walk among the New Yorkers none seem to be aware of the hysteria being caused globally by this fool with bad hair. He has become a laughing stock around the world, but his moronic rhetoric has caused rifts and fractions with other world leaders like it could easily destabilise the peace we enjoy on a global scale. Russia upset, Arab nations disgusted, and Europe thinking that surely the American people would not to let this bozo into the White House. A phony, his past, says one thing and has the opposite in his next speech. Nothing more than a reality trash TV star, but he has managed to persuade lowest common denominator of racist, White trash Americans to follow him and bully anyone who opposes. I fear that tonight in New York could be the boiling point for when America loses all political credibility.

The reality TV news that has now become dominated by Facebook with fake videos and lies, I feel that the owners of the land of the fake personas has had a dollar bet that they can sway this evil into power.

6

I enter a photo shop and buy an ID card kit. No one sees me buy it, no one looks to see what he or she are selling, I leave and set to a nearby coffee shop that has a passport booth next to it. A worker in an electrician's outfit is standing by the machine. I tell him I am repairing the machine I need to photograph someone to check all is working. He looks a little like me, not much, but enough. His name is Karl. He's like most Americans happy friendly and just happy to help and sits in the Booth as I pretend to be outside monitoring. Flash the camera takes Karl's photo I ask him to wait. I load the machine again as the picture did not work, I tell him. Karl politely sits patiently back into the seat and again the flash goes off on the camera again as the first picture I've taken arrives without Karl knowing. I pocket the picture. I then asked Karl to exit the booth. I have pocketed the picture first taken and then the second picture arrives and I hand to Karl, who is grateful, as he quite likes the way he looks. Karl walks back to his work aimlessly looking at his picture, not realising he has just given his face to my invisible mission.

Sat once again in the coffee shop I take out the picture of Karl, one of the four photographs to make the new security pass I will need for tonight. I laughed to myself is the names I have chosen at random as I walked down the Boulevard of New York I'm now electrician Karl Perkins. I set off downtown to pick up my case I left in the snooker hall three months ago; I walk past the assembly room that will hold tonight's Rally.

I stop unnoticed outside and see, unloading a van, sits a man with speakers and a PA for the presidential elect to

44

voice his rhetoric over. I casually walk over to the van and with my mobile take a few candid shots of the company logo and look around to notice in doing so I have remained invisible. I then see the man sitting next to PA struggling with a large speaker and rush to his assistance. Within seconds I find his name is Dave and he owns the company, I help him in with the speaker and in no time there I am inside the Hall and walking on the stage where my target will be speaking.

I laugh at how tight the security is, but as the Invisible Man I just walk in and have full access. A security guard comes over and I ask him what time kick off will be? He tells me his name is Pete and I say hi back, I am Karl, and establish he will be on duty at Gate B tonight. As we chat Dave passes by and I call to him to say that if he wants be able to help move the big speakers in. Dave raises his hand and exits. I ask Pete where the main TV gallery is going to be and see it being rigged. Enough information gained and I exit, retreating back to the invisibility of the street. I clock Gate B and see a small side door to the TV station gallery. I smile and think to myself not all missions are this easy.

On the street I see a pretty girl with long brown hair below her shoulders offer a pizza to a homeless girl. The homeless girl smiles and is so gracious in her gratitude I am once more humbled by what we can achieve and us humans. As I turn and see the pretty brunette pass me she smiles to herself and I realise she has done that before. I catch a reflection of me in a shop window smiling and remember Isobel in Exeter.

I tell you reader as an aside I often ask the homeless if they would like something to eat and arrive with a

Chinese lunchbox or Indian takeaway. The homeless are always really grateful, humble, never ask for more, and as to the smile they give you as you walk away, well it cannot be measured. I look to my mobile and see it is already 11:30am. I quicken my pace and get to the snooker hall. It is just in 42nd Street. I walk with conviction and a new found faith in the American people thanks to one pretty girl and there is an extra stride in my step.

I arrive at the snooker hall above a pawnshop. No surprise as much has been won or lost above. I enter with my locker key and sit in the corner unnoticed with a cup of Joe and open my snooker cue case I had retrieved from the locker.

I had the case made for me and in it it has a portrait photo printer and cables set up to tiny tablet and cards to print on that can be laminated by a small laminator I had added. I silently plug the electrics into a cleaner's plug on the wall and bingo we are live. The socket is next to a coffee table and I use the cable to plug in my mobile. On the tablet I then am able to crop the electric company logo and print onto card with my picture and new name, as new ID card is printed I use a cutter in the box that came with ID kit and formatted cards, I stick Karl's photo in place, the logo is in place, sharpie pen in name, and seal under lamination pouch then laminate.

Within five minutes I went from Invisible to Karl Perkins working for Dave and his AV Company. I place the cables and extra ID card kit bought earlier into the snooker cue box, and return it to the locker. I exit out the snooker room door and start to return to Joe's in Queens. Walking back to Queens to get a subway I start to pass delegates for tonight's big event. The atmosphere has

46

changed so much and it reminiscent of walking with away fans at a highly charged local football match. All the delegates strutting their stuff and already threatening people walking by. When I say people, I mean anyone not white or an obvious fellow supporter. I watch from my invisible viewpoint and see how these mindless morons parade as if they were as happy to be sports fans as they would be members of the KKK, and then I see it; an emblem of a Grand Dragon.

I had not seen that emblem since I was on a mission in Georgia. They were a ferociously hardline chapter and boasted many Black and Jewish killings. I had heard the rumours that my mission target was a Klansman sympathiser, but now I was convinced.

Reader, it has always been a small world, and I suddenly recognised an old foe. Back in Georgia he was a local judge, or ex-judge, as he is on the run for his involvement in raping and murdering seven black girls aged 7 - 14. He was said to have died in a car crash in Utah, but there was no mistaking that tattoo on his wrist of the emblem of the Grand Dragon. My mission had just doubled and often we have to make choices of what our priorities are. Sometimes we are lucky, and this was one of those moments when my two missions became one. As I followed them out of the subway back onto the street I see them walk into a tall gaudy tower hotel, with the decor and style of a blind lunatic who had read nothing but the works of the Marquis de Sade, twenty-four seven.

As I relax as had not been noticed I almost bump into the security team from my initial mission at a second entrance. I cross the road to enter the hotel. There is so

47

much ostentatious red and gold that it would be hard to focus on anybody in the lobby, this is an Invisible Man's dream. I was able to get close enough to hear conversations and not be noticed. I stood open to be seen, which is why those looking never see me. An old trick as they look to see who is hiding and not the obvious.

I see the Grand dragon enter the lift with one of his security team. He looks me in the face as the doors close I smile at him. I wanted him to be unsure that someone had seen him, it was daft, but his holier than thou untouchable attitude galled me. I watched the lift rise with the occupants inside. It was one of those interior lifts where you can be seen inside and lucky for me as I can see the occupants exit and then saw them walk to the third door on the right of the lift. I was in the lift on the opposite side following up. I take the lift back down one I had secured a room number as all the hotel doors had huge numbering. This hotel seemed to have been designed by a colour blind cretin who was also short sighted. They were on the twelve floor and I felt fate had entered the scene as I watch my hit number two enter room 1321. I see a maid cart outside room 1221 below. I head back up and without her noticing as she exits slip in behind her and I am in 1221. Above me the most hideous excuse for a human, wanted and yet able to walk with ease around the city of New York.

I am in the room and see a balcony door and we have a terrace. Looking out at the amazing view I take out my mobile and attach a telephoto lens attachment and gingerly exit to climb to the terrace above. It is relatively easy and wonder, who designed this cat burglars heaven? Within a few seconds I am safely creeping onto 1321 balcony. I see someone sat in a high chair with his back to me talking to the Dragon. They are having an animated conversation. The French windows are slightly ajar. Then the fake looking blonde hair is unmistakable and I realise my mission has far greater consequences than first thought, I have to act fast.

I have a detachable microphone that can clip audio to my mobile. I remember buying this phone and having to be taught how to make a phone call. I remember the whole sales pitch was about you can make a movie on your mobile and the sales clerk look at me as if I was an alien when asked about the phone call making capabilities. Timing was unbelievable as two security guards suddenly stood with their backs to the French doors blocking my view; in fact they were blocking me from being detected. I literally stood behind them with mic clipped onto frame and my head between theirs filming. No one noticed the third head.

As I listen to what I am recording I realise that I have the ammunition, no the rocket launcher to blow two evil cretins out of the water. Then I smile as I realise this hideous hotel is owned by my first hit. He really has no class or taste.

The Dragon is getting agitated, as he wants to come out from hiding and is demanding Presidential elect businessman to sort it out. I listen as my hit explains that once he is in office they will plant information crushing his conviction, an eight-figure payment for compensation and that he would be involved in all new construction works and oversea through new company set up in his name the workforce.

They laugh, as they will have the Blacks and Jews working for them just like back in the good old days. They agree to keep their associations quiet as not to let anyone know as it could damage their master plan. Then Invisible Man gold, my first hit stands and warmly embraces the Dragon. And is if on queue looks to camera to say,

" Listen my old friend, after I whip up this mob into a frenzy I will have all opponents campaigns trashed, and you and I will rule the world Buddy! "

The two stand side by side and both look straight at me holding the camera and then to each other. Then they look back as if they saw something. They look as if to say they saw three heads and now just two. I hear a commotion and the guards rush onto the balcony and I am gone.

" No one here Boss ", I hear one say and the French doors are closed.

" Must have been section in double glazing diffracting images," Says the other.

I am on the balcony below and walking into room 1221 with mic, mobile and life in tact. All I had to do now was implement my plan, but as you may realise Reader the plan is an organic thing, sometimes we have no idea how things will unfold, but we adapt to the environment.

Remember if you wish to follow to be an Invisible then a mission is not set with any real plans, just an objective, things happen and you have to adapt. Oh, and not for the feint hearted.

7

I remember a night in Angola with another Invisible Man called Roland. He was Hungarian and helped me highlight a British Prime Minister's son attempts to overthrow a country.

We followed him together and managed to thwart his attempt and also my mission was to expose a corrupt African General. The latter was easy as they are all uneducated idiot thugs who forget bullying is not a sign of power. We managed both at the same time as always these people feel they are above the law; too clever to ever be caught. Sadly, the British PM, she was so corrupt that the trail leading to successful prosecution failed as there was no way anyone could believe the truth as it was just so fantastical.

The same was for my second hit the Dragon and the Presidential Candidate. They had made a secret pact that reminded me of my wise friend Roland. Roland said to me that if you want to keep a secret a secret, then the first mouth you should keep shut is your own. Roland was a humble man, yet greater in stature as a human being than either of these appalling tyrants would ever be.
As I exited the lobby one of the security guards sees me. I smile and exit. He thinks I am a fan of his boss. If he sees me tonight remaining invisible will be difficult.

As easy as it was to film my mission target I know it is just as easy to loose my invisibility. I hope that that guard is backstage and decide I am going to have to walk through the front door.

I was now heading to Queens and the bar was already buzzing. All opponents to my mission and his campaign gathered in the bar. I was among friends. They had congregated to watch the televised event live. Many were in good spirits laughing at his ludicrous statements of how he will make America great again, and others pensive and nervous as they see the danger he brings.

You see Reader, as in the JFK book he notices how England sat by and watched Hitler's rise, they failed to see Hitler's true intent until exposed and then nations rose to oppose and overthrow. It took a six-year war to end that costly mistake, but with social media and instant news I felt we the Invisible should be able to make an instant hit. For you Reader are the people, we are all on a mission to make our world a better place for all and why you must keep this journal safe is because the powers that rule and oppress would never want us to realise that if we stand, we would not stand alone. I often wonder what and even who were all the previous Invisibles that made such sacrifices. A guy that knew the Chinese student standing in front of the tank in Tiananmen Square recruited me. Today his courage will rise and using all my powers to honour him, using the press and instant media affiliations, even though there is no real free press anymore, the press will have to show or see their own demise the fall of this Neanderthal political monster. The exciting part of this mission is that I have to make this happen live, with the world's press watching, so that they cannot spin or delete or try to deflect the information just flashed across the globe.

The scary part is if I fail what I have does not get seen, well here I go up to my room to prepare to make sure I get the world to see the truth as it is and that the proof I have cannot be denied.

In the room I hear the people below, many discussing tonight's show. It is as if a circus has come to town. The main talk is how all cannot believe that my target has got this far. At first it was a joke, then offending all the Mexicans, Latin Americans, Women and his tirade of abuse continues to Britain, China, Muslims - a whole religion! He then is proud to prove he is the misogynist man on the planet. He manages to describe his own daughter as hot and how he would bang her if she was not his daughter.

He even dismisses a female reporter as she only got the job, as she is attractive. A remark that followed her intellectually running circles round him.

As for anyone questioning what he says or asks him a question he cannot answer, he dismisses him or her by saying they are trying to trick him into a dumb answer. For eighty percent of the American people I feel they would regret if it were them saying everything he says, yet he is the leader in the race to the White House. He conquers by offending each sector, bullying and pitching one society against another, and make them feel that the bigotry he spouses would come true if they did not vote for any other candidate.

News teams and satirists, local and world celebrities campaign for his demise, but he just grows stronger. The uneducated, the disenfranchised people of America, many who never vote now decide he is the anti-politician vote, they are tired of the career Presidents that never relate to them. I look at the outgoing fella and realise that he was one of the best for a long time and will be revered in years to come as one of the greats.

The world's press is assembled for if this rally happens with same gusto as previous, this lunatic, megalomaniac, all the world shuns, could be in the White House race. The damage he has already done in the global political arena is immeasurable. Russia now on alert, NATO worried, and even the Arab, Mexican, Black, Jewish, Liberal countries even are concerned about the stability of the world. Concerned not the best word Reader, but the world are seeing the Americans as a major diplomatic problem. And I still cannot laugh at the events as he is only saying he wants to be President; the fear comes if this idiot savant ever does make it to the White House. He feels everyone should have nuclear weapons for starters.

As a country between America and Europe and its partners we see the Americans travelling on our soil, walking our streets, and realise thanks to this man they are walking targets for terrorists and Yank hating countries in the world. And there are more countries disliking America everyday due to this fool. I really mean this sincerely America, if you vote this moron in to one of the highest positions in the world today you will be signing the death warrants for many of your fellow Americans overseas. Any American wanting to travel to see Paris, Rome, London, Madrid, Venice, Sydney...... the list goes on and on, well just forget it. You would not be safe. We are horrified to think that years ago people put up signs no Blacks or Irish; well I feel that the signs will go up 'No Americans' as people do not want their hotels or restaurants bombed.

So Reader, a little about the Americans to those who have not met them on mass. They are wonderful. Meeting Americans travelling or living among them as I have in many of the different States you will be hard pushed to find a kinder, smarter or giving people. A huge nation that is often wrongly judged by the actions of a few. Over 300 million live in harmony, it is not perfect, but where is, yet the world only ever reads about the stupidity of the few. Just one hundred religious fanatics in smallsville America spouting vile rhetoric and all Americans tarred with the same brush. My target has galvanised so many that the world tonight watches. New York city is the new square in Munich. Will the American people fall victim to a false prophet and see that this tin God is only out for himself. I now have the only silver bullet to bring him down. My aim is true,

My heart is ready, and my will to succeed against all the odds has never been more resilient. You see Reader, I am the Invisible Man, my duty is to ensure that the minority is heard over the jack-boots of tyrannical, self-obsessed narcissists like my dangerous target speaking tonight. His speech of hate, division and accusations will see him possibly in one of the most powerful hot seats in the world. His politics of lies and fear, bullying the impressionable uneducated mass of followers into taking this great nation into the wilderness and make America the most soul less place on the planet. America, unwelcome anywhere else on the planet and a country ridiculed as the land of the dumb instead of the free.

8

I hear a beep on my mobile. One of my Facebook profiles switches on, it is from Barbara, a fanatic who is ecstatic about tonight as she is a believer. She writes that she feels my target will make America great again. Looking at her Facebook page I can easily see that she is a shallow, homophobic, racist, who blames everyone in the world for her being an uneducated, jobless waste of space. The minute my target started spouting on about Mexicans are all rapists and drug dealers taking good honest hard working Americans' jobs she was in. This thirty-nine year old drug taking drunk, living in a trailer, on welfare and with three children from three fathers who she cannot even remember meeting, this redneck is overjoyed that she can be a part of something that blames others for their own plight or downfall, and not have to take any responsibility themselves. I read a few posts, then start to delete and unfriend those that I followed to monitor, as when the shit hits the fan, one of these idiots could indirectly make me visible.

So I am dressed in workman's gear, and exit the bar without even being noticed. Even Joe is oblivious to my passing him. I am invisible and on my way.

I catch the subway and an eerie gloom descends on New York as the real New Yorkers head home and away from the rally. They are too ashamed to be associated with tonight's event. They are horrified that in their city the world watches America fall into the pit of depravity. The subway exit is full of rednecks and the atmosphere is charged with white supremacists ready to erupt into violence. Like two local teams in a play off in a local derby where the neighbours are ready to fight and go to war on themselves. There is a chant heard in the distance, I realise it is from the subway platforms below. The platform heaving with bodies, drunken women, already falling over in badly fitting clothes. Men with hats saying National Rifle Association and War on Terror. All talking in unintelligible dialects, and all feeling they have a right to own a gun and shoot any Nigger, Muslim or Jew to protect their property.

I remember asking a guy once why he needed a gun and he said to protect his property. I remember laughing as he lived in a run down trailer that made a place described as squalor look like a palace and thought to myself looking at this total jerk, 'Buddy, the only reason anyone would break into your house is to steal your gun!' Let's face it, and talking to all the dumbest Americans that are living, if they had no gun then no one would even think of paying these bums a visit.

But many of these are the local guard for my mission. My target has surrounded himself in the vile and the dangerous majority of lemmings that look for a cause where they are vindicated for being dumb. They will follow people like my target without thought, many have no capacity for thought, without questioning anything he says. They are a lost generation looking to follow a cause wherever he goes, people of no importance who now have a cause, and the cause is to make America great again. By any means and that means bullying and beating up anyone who stands up to question or oppose my hit for tonight. But remember I have a double hit and as I walk I look around carefully managing to blend in and disappear invisible.

The enormity of the situation hits me and I realise that this mission has grown even larger than first feared. Not just about making sure America stops a hate generating monster or saving America, but about saving world peace.

I pass loyal fans saying they are looking for terrorists as they may be trying to infiltrate and kill them all. I think of Samir and Suzie and hope they are tucked up safely away from here. A Putin doll burns as anti-Russian chants of 'commi-bastards die' is heard and cheered. But then one once says that Russian women are hot and all agree before going back to death to commies chants. There is even a group warning that all Muslims are Communists and there is a double threat; whilst my fear is reaffirmed with many agreeing that they had not thought of that and shortly 'death to all commi-Muslims' is shouted out from within the mob. The talk of weapons of mass destruction lead me to realise the only weapon of mass destruction we have to worry about is the weapon of mass destruction that is their misguided vote blowing up their country from within.

But this is a warning America to yourselves. Those that know this is happening and look to fight against, look beyond what is happening and re read what I just wrote:

They are a lost generation looking to follow a cause wherever he goes, people of no importance who now have a cause, and the cause is to make America great again.

You have created a lost generation from your own greed and idealistic American Dream where those that cannot make it are cast aside. The numbers have grown considerably and now you have an army internally of disenchanted people looking for any messiah who would

58

talk to them. Numbers that have engulfed and overwhelmed your country. The outgoing President has tried to show help to those and shown you how to be generous to make change, but you still live on fake Facebook statuses and the world is great for you. You must start to change the fortunes of those that cannot do it alone.

I see the venue and make my way towards Gate B. With my identity badge in place, my bag of tools in hand, I hope to see Pete and slip by unnoticed. At the door I am again in luck, Pete is by the door in charge of people going in and out. Then as if trying to assist me the mob help my entrance.

A group of demonstrators protest behind police barriers and within seconds the atmosphere changes. Hatred charges the air, and we see mounted police charge between the opposing groups. A Gay and Lesbian group behind the police face thirty to one numbers looking to literally kill them. I cannot, but stand and watch with pride as again those standing there making a visible protest against this mob are those that are always the vulnerable. The LGBT face courageously bigotry everyday and yet stand tall wearing the hatred as a badge in defiance. It looks as if the mob is going to get to them; the police seem to look as if they do not want to get hurt for just some queers. Then a miracle happens from behind the LGBT arrives a huge mass of Black, Hispanic, Muslim and true New York liberals ready to stand side by side. This my reader is a sight truly to behold. All is still as I stand and look with pride at my fellow man, visible and courageous in the face of adversity, standing together as one to protect the weak and those at risk. This Reader is the true American.

The mob suddenly seeing numbers even up slow up and back up from the fight. They just chant obscenities and make out they would fight. The protestors stand tall and their peaceful demonstration would of made the great Gandhi proud.

I see out the corner of my eye Pete, flustered and seem totally stressed out. He too is in charge of Gate B and completely over evaluating the situation. I wave at him and he waves back, he has no idea who I am, but because he waved two attendants rusher me through. He is confused and in true Invisible Man mode I bowl over without hesitation, hold up my fake ID that he glances at briefly, at which point the mob start to shout angrily at again. To be honest as I passed through the mob I shouted, 'look out Muslims protesting.' Within seconds the desired effect on the masses supporting the Target reacted exactly as required giving me the diversion to use on Pete.

"Looks like you've got your hands full here Pete?" Pete looks at me confused. I hold up my fake ID. "Karl Perkins sound engineer".

"Oh yes mate, sorry didn't recognise you there ". Pete then guides me into the building and I see there is a guard on the door to TV gallery.

"Right, sorry had to come back as cable missing linking sound to picture for TV, they'd be looking for scalps if I don't fit this ", I say and Pete grabs an Access All Areas badge. "Sorry you'll need this Karl ", he says and hands me the badge.

Pete walks briskly to the door to the gallery and gets me past the guard.

"Karl Perkins, this guy needs to get to sound links and pronto. Sorry got to leave you with Eddie here Karl as it's going to be a long night I fear. Glad when this bozo leaves town. " And with that Eddie opens the door and Pete goes back to his walkie talkie.

I walk into the booth past all the security with my new wristband and past the director shouting at his assistant to find out why camera three is not working.

I see my chance, "Just on it." and slip behind the main desk. It has actually all been too easy.

To be honest Reader you will find that most missions are easy to gain access as easily as this has been as those that should be watching are always looking for people that stand out. I am nobody, ordinary. When you become part of the crowd you disappear and yes, it is then we are invisible.

I wire up a transmitter to the over ride on the console and switch on my app on my mobile. All the lights on my app light up and suddenly luck has it camera three clicks on. I exit to have a big pat on the back from the director. Soon I am out of the room, down the stairs and walking into the main room.

I find an emergency exit and stand close to that. I already know this leads to the main street and is used for TV cables that the alarm has been disabled. I basically saw the cable wire and it is obvious to the trained eye.

I was at a press conference in Dubai and helping a young Indian Family escape a Sheik's employment, when he was busy with Heads of State, we used similar escape route, I do not know if you remember a case of families abused and held captive by Arab Leaders whose power and money knew no boundaries. Rumours of this one Sheik's abuse of those in his service became well known, after that mission and the following press call from the family that changed for a while. The Sheik in question had a fishing accident in the dessert and was killed by a spear gun. Yes, even washing their dirty laundry they do it in the Arabic States in such an unfazed way that they do not care how improbably the way it is done, they feel they will never be questioned.

The Indian Family were whisked to the United States and disappeared. It was interesting to note that shortly afterwards what was to be an extremely tricky trade negotiation went through without a hitch.

The crowd was building to capacity and it was funny to see we were not in seats, but corralled into roped off areas. I was squashed in hidden by a group of what I feared were Klansmen. But my mission was in full swing, no going back now and all Invisible Men and Women know the risks. I smile knowing that the cameras will be on me soon enough and they will also protect me when needed.

Suddenly a row of huge black men enter and stand in front of me right next to the Klansmen. The Klansmen look and upon seeing the size of the Black men realise they are hemmed in and unable to move or get out. I smile at my newfound Black friend, as the rednecks look terrified. I realised this was another blessing in disguise.

9 The circus begins as the hall is literally packed. A fire officer's nightmare, but then again not a tragedy that would be mounted for long. When I said the circus begins I wasn't joking. There is a warm up act of a racist comic whose first joke contains the words an Arab, A Jew and A Pakistani walk into Yankee Stadium. The big black man in front of me looks round in disgust and then looks down at me.

" Don't worry," I said, " I am sure he'll get round to saying niggers soon."

He looks at me and then breaks into a really thundering laugh. So loud that all turn as does the comic who sees who is laughing, struck with fear as I reckon his next joke is colour challenged and starts to fluff his lines. He carries on with a really sexist joke about a woman owing her husband a blowjob and then shouts, " Any commies in the house? " And is if coming on to save the day he is interrupted by a big breasted blonde model who is in a costume far to small for a chest like hers. She is introduced as Wanda Phillem and all cheer, well the rednecks cheer. I mean Reader, this woman was in a top and no bra so when she walked it looked like a ferret chasing a rabbit around a plastic sack. Wanda is to sing the national anthem. Well I use the word sing in its most liberal way. One of my target's bimbos as he runs a pageant called 'Trailer Queen'. I think he is married to one of the winners.

But it matters not how bad she sang the mob sang along with her shouting the words. Next to me the rednecks did well up until the fourth line of the song and then made noises as they didn't even know the words. The black guys suddenly take over and they are amazing. Who were they, 'Boys To Men' twenty years on?

One thing the Americans have in spades, and I do not mean that as a pun, is their incredible patriotism. Other countries have fanatics too, but none like the American Patriots and possibly we Brits who also sing our national anthem, well also all the European countries and I am realising this is a crap analogy, but the Americans love their country. Standing in a mob of hatred and fractions ready to go to war with each other all stops to sing as one the Star Spangled Banner.

With this I feel how proud a nation America is and that it already is a great nation as I watch in an out of body experience the pride in the room to be American. I watch mainly trailer trash as they are called, the worst degenerates of American society, hardly any Asians or minorities, but loads of white uneducated America singing, badly in most cases, and that included Wanda who has the audience transfixed with her heaving bosom, all proud and then I hear the sweetest voices of the black men in front of me. The black men standing proud and tall, my God these guys were giants, hands on hearts, singing in great harmony as one and I wonder if they know where they are? I mean one row in front of them is the Klan and my second target.

The crowd roars as the song ends and in comes a clown dressed as a Russian and prat falls on the stage. The mob love it and cheer. I am wondering what the Kremlin thinks of this? Then a Mexican as a string puppet and an Arab guy with a toilet roll on his head as a Muslim.

Could this get any worse? Yes on comes my target to huge cheers. He kicks the Russian in the backside and he rushes off the stage, then shouts at the Arab actor, "Hey shit head, get off my stage!" All the crowd roars with laughter and cheer.

The mob goes crazy. They all laugh and repeat to each other the joke Hey Shit Head, he has a toilet roll on his head and laugh even harder.

My target holds up his hand and all goes quiet.

"Hey Gringo?" he shouts not realising Gringo is what Mexican movie characters used to call white people, "Hey Gringo, build me that wall."

A broom is then given to my target and he proceeds to sweep the Mexican off the stage and all cheer as if this was the greatest thing they have ever seen. All except my row of black giants. I am literally too gobsmacked to react and as the row of black giants in front of me stand stoic not moving I sense that something else is going down. I just hope that a second diversion does not scupper my plan. A plan hatched on the go, I grant you, often the best missions are, adapt and move as we say. Most of the best plans have an element of winging it. As when all hits the fan, the police will be looking with the authorities for the series of different men that were all then the visible men and innocent of all crime that the Invisible can leave without a trace. Well I certainly hope this is the case tonight.

Well my dear Reader, all this will become crystal clear as you read on. This mission was never complex and we have a saying used by many Invisible Men and that is just Kiss it. Short for Keep It Simple Stupid. What may seem to many, as an elaborate plan often is just a little smoke and mirrors with an app off a mobile. This mission was no different except that on this mission I was actually in the cage with the lions. When I poke them I will be seen by all. I put on my baseball cap and have coloured contact lenses in, no idea why, just thought be good at the time, and it may help add to the confusion.

My new black friend watches me put on my cap. As stated my Boston Red Sox cap. I look at him.

"Yankees Fan?"

"Hell no! Dodgers," he replies. His friend turns to say that they are Yankees fans and I explain that I like the colour red and one laughs.

"Australians."

Yes yet again the British accent to most of America is Australian.

"In about twenty minutes all will go mad in here. Stick close Aussie and you should be OK", he says to me.

I smile and tap his shoulder. He looks back at me and I ask him to bend down, well he was a giant. I whisper in his ear. His colleague watches.

"Hi, names Karl Perkins, if you can hold off the fireworks until I have done my thing there may be no need for any madness you may have planned." He looks back at me and I whisper back.

"I am going to ruin this chump without one action of violence."

The one watching nods to ask his friend what I said. They confer and laugh. The one watching leans towards me and I lean towards him.

"What do you need?" he asks.

"Just the mic," I say and he laughs.

"Hey Tony, we got to get the Aussie the Mic."

I smile and he looks back at me.

"You'll get the mic then after that it could get a little mad in here."

10

As my target gets into full swing it is obvious he has strayed off script as he constantly managing to contradict himself. He starts off making this country great again, then dividing communities, and blaming first the immigrants for downfall of everyone's way of life, then saying he comes from proud immigrant family, then blames the opponents friends in the banks for downfall and finally terrorists.

The mob goes wild. He is a genius. Why did no one ever say this before as all are in a trance listening to his every word, not understanding anything he says and then cheering and nodding approval.

I laugh as he starts on the Chinese and spot an Asian group in front looking as if they think he must be picking on them. There is suddenly tension and I see first hand just how dangerous this moron is. I watch our illustrious cretin on stage touch his ear as obviously someone had shouted in his ear' No, Change track!' And then to try to make a seamless transition states that he would no longer trade with China and everything would be made in the USA. All the mob cheer and start chanting USA USA USA. As they chant he holds his earpiece again and as if to say to camera 'What?' 'They love me'. It is then I see him touch his ear again and as if a flash of brilliance has hit him and in defiance to the voices in his head saying, 'NO!!!!!!' he turns to the Asians in the audience and addresses them direct.

" I see many Asian friends here tonight and I know that you have fled China to this great land. Away from being abused, having to kill your second born babies, daughters mainly as you only want sons, and I am proud of my relationships with the Chinese fighting against oppression."

The crowd goes wild and again he laps up the adulation.

"We are Japanese," shouts one of the group.

"Exactly," he replies and without pause follows up with, " Of course not all Mexicans are rapists, but I think I have made myself clear on that one."

I stood there in amazement, as he had no idea of what he was saying other than to be playing to areas of the crowd, who would in return unexplainably cheer in agreement. The most upsetting thing was to look to see who was cheering and to be confronted by a sea of men and women raising their arms and in doing so their ill fitting clothes, exposing their cracks in their backsides; it was like a Mexican wave of builder's bum.

Another ten minutes past and still not one moment did he talk about how realistically he would make America great again. He just played to the crowd, fed their fears and blamed others for their situations and said he could make America great again. He kept saying it, but I still have no idea how he thinks he will do this. Soon people started shouting, "I love you," and he starts blowing kisses. This was a political rally like no other. Suddenly a small voice was heard shouting dissent. A young black girl in her twenties. She was boo'd and crowd confrontation was scary to say the least. This woman was so courageous and yet I was scared for her.

"Calm down, my people, calm down," is heard from the stage as our speaker strutting towards the side the girl is on.

"I think we have another opposition stool pigeon here and I think you all know my feeling on this matter."

The crowd starts to chant 'drag her out', ' Beat the shit out of her'. My black guys start to move. I see a girl with an audience microphone and my moment has come. Grabbing the mic I shout and it is turned on. The whole place goes silent and the black guys shield me from being seen.

The crowd slowly shouts, 'Who's talking?' and I am invisible.

"Stop the violence." I shout. Then a calm is more of confusion as the mob look to the stage for direction for they have no idea how to deal with the voice coming from the sky.

"Excuse me sir," I start, "I am from overseas coming to see your show here".

"This ain't a show, this is us Americans fighting for our country!" He shouts back. I look to see my target strutting about on stage like a peacock with his dodgy haircut.

"Well we overseas are growing ever so worried by this violent rhetoric you espouse against anyone that has the nerve to disagree with you. You offer no debate, no voice of reason or argue with any intelligence."

I notice an army of thugs trying to find me and retrieve the mic, but we are live on TV and all look confused. My Black giant looks to me and says, "Carry on brother this is fun."

"So whom are you aligning with to make America great again? Who? The Klan?" as the brothers all turn to look at me. I toss the mic onto the stage and he and everyone dive for cover. There is a silence and seeing it is the mic my target gets up off the floor and kicks the mic away. The Black Giants link arms to protect me, but the idiots looking go into the wrong pen section.

"Hey Aussie you are good," says my new friend protecting me.

"And I think in five minutes things are going to become even more fun." I reply.

Without hesitation this uncompromising businessman with the White House in his sights decides to answer off cue card, off his speech, and true to the man he is he decides to talk without thinking. I had broken down the last layer to expose him.

"So again my enemies try to slander my good name. I am about to give power to the KKK? Really? That they are all my friends? That anyone that would argue with me would be shot? Lynched?" The audience laughs. "Please? I am a man of my word, a man of principle, and listen Buddy, listen to the American people, and see and hear from all these great folks here tonight in New York, and all over the country, the real Americans the true patriots are behind me." There is a huge cheer after nearly every sentence.

"Buddy, I speak all the hard working Americans saying no more."

The crowd shouts in unison as if in a trance, "No More! "

"No more are we going to let the Mexicans cross our borders, no more loss of trade to the slanty-eyed Chinese, no more buying over priced oil from some dirty Arab. No sir, no more. "

The crowd is in a frenzy, and going wild chanting No More! My black giant looks at me, and grins, "Hey sucker you ain't winning this one."

"Just a few seconds more, " I smile and reply.

"Am I a racist? Hell no! A Tyrant? Hell no! I am a man of the people!" he shouts as if he just won the lottery and then it happened. Everything fell in line and I pushed the go button on my app on my mobile and the edited piece from earlier hit the big screens all over the venue. Watching the target spin and look thinking what's this gave me the greatest joy, but watching the crowd turn to silence was just nirvana. Standing there as all his supporters, campaign managers, workers looked at me and my body guards stand defiantly, me holding my mobile aloft in the air, watching their big grins on their faces turn from as if to say that put you in your place to then watch and see their beloved leader doing a deal with a Grand Dragon, a convicted Grand Dragon as I had subtitled that was at the rally and that Pete and the police should come arrest him, I look at my new best friends, my black giants wetting themselves with laughter I just smile and say, " That gentlemen is how an Invisible Man does it."

The conversation of how the target will secretly clear the Dragon's name with false evidence once in power and give him all works where he can hire niggers cheap and lynch any that complain as long as done quietly, he just wants 50% of the profits.

I hear screams over the silence from the target shouting to turn it off, but the damage is done.

We hear on the screen our man on the stage with his back to camera shake hands with the Dragon and say as if on cue,

"So keep a low profile my old friend. I will get you a new identity and put you in charge of an anti-American committee, your own commission, you'll be a billionaire like me, just use the boys to make sure the liberals vote our way at the polling stations or not vote at all."

As my wannabe President hugs the Dragon and announces that he is as much a Klansman as he ever was, they will get all major contracts once he is in power the mob turn and start to shout.

Then the former strutting peacock running for President is seen turning to camera and looking straight down the lens. It could not of been better.

The screen splits as I edited and we see my two targets shaking hands and a voice over for my friend Pete.

"Officer Pete, in the auditorium is this Grand Dragon, wanted for rape and murder of seven young girls aged 7-14 years old. Arrest him for us please as we all want America to be great again, but happy to realise that

America is already great and that now we, the people in this rally want you to help us end this hatred clouding our vision, for today we stand as one unified country, united, all encompassing, compassionate and brave, United States of America."

"What the hell is this you piece of shit? " his on stage mic still on.

Yes that was the least of my targets worries as the furious Dragon shouts that he'll get him for this and exposes exactly where he is and the good people of America lift him up from his Klansmen and body serve him across their heads to the police waiting.

The mob starts booing and throwing banners of support once held high onto the stage as the false prophet runs off stage.

The site of the Grand Dragon and his men being dragged over heard to the police is cheered all the way and when arrested the audience give a mighty cheer.

The Black bodyguards protecting me smile and turn round to look at me, but I have gone. I have already made my escape. I am invisible again and make my way to my exit route.

Suddenly a disgruntled supporter bars my exit route. It was Dougal. He places his hand on my shoulder, "That book was excellent, thanks for the read. You going out this way? I will happily hold the door for you my friend." I smile and exit.

Within seconds I am in the street and heading to the subway. You see reader as an Invisible Man you have to often hope for a little luck and believe in the people. They may not always get it or see what is happening, but once seen they come together to stand united against all that is wrong. I see LGBT supporters crying and hugging each other as thousands leave the rally and some walk over and shake their hand. I am interested to see how the final part of my exit plan worked at Joe's.

I enter Joe's place and a party is in full swing. Joe sees me and asks, "Alfredo where you been? You must have a doppelganger, look, I look with my own eyes and think it is Alfredo and then they say everybody looking for electrician Karl Perkins. This Karl Perkins he could be you doppelganger."

"Doppelganger?" I reply and as Joe happily say yes he notices a beautiful girl at the bar.

"Excuse me Alfredo. I think have just seen my next ex-wife." Joe laughs and rushes over to the girl. I see the police enter and on screen my face as Karl Perkins. They have a photo of me and it seems Joe in his excitement called to say that was me.

I look to see I still have my identity badge on and quickly remove and place it in my coat pocket on the stairs as I dash up to my room. My bag is packed and ready to go as I exit via the back window.

11

Obviously Reader you will realise I have done this before, but that is another story. As I exit past the bar window I see Joe laughing with the police and see him say that he was mistaken, Alfredo is not Karl Perkins. Joe just wanted to be seen with the guy that bought down America's Hitler, plus what a publicity stunt for Joe.

Walking down the streets of Queens trying to find a cab it suddenly dawns on me I have nowhere to stay. I put my hand in my wallet and there is the answer as I find Marjorie's card. I walk into another bar and call her. She is in and it is only a short drive away. She did say pop by and it seems both she and Giselle are in alone watching a movie. Seems this has been the luckiest mission ever.

As the cab whisks me to Marjorie's I note it is only 10pm and stop off to buy Proscecco. Champagne is over rated and to be honest not as good. I buy myself some American champagne and we carry on. Driving the driver tells me of his kid want to go to Disneyland. He seems to be a good dad and find five hundred dollars from the casino win I will not necessarily spend as leave in a few days and hand it to him as a tip. Don't ask why, but felt really good. Reaching in to pay I find Karl Perkin's ID in my pocket. I had made a mistake of not throwing the ID away, but now it would be my saviour. I tap on the cab driver's window.

"Hey Buddy, some guy left his pass in the back." I hand it to him and he looks to exit.

As I arrive I see the two girls waiting for me at the apartment window most of New York is out celebrating as the news of my hit has filtered through.

The girls are half dressed as I enter and say that they are taking me to a party. I reflect on the day and night and see my face on the TV behind the two girls as they chat to me. I hear a reward for $5,000 for any information to the discovery of finding Karl Perkins. I am sure the Taxi driver will realise much later what he has and get some reward.

The girls look stunning and they are actually just in their underwear. I smile and ask,

"Have I come too soon?" and Marjorie pulls me towards her and says, "We hope not."

My invisibility in tact and never making it to the party I can say that Marjorie and Giselle were the greatest hosts I have ever stayed with.

You see Reader, Invisible Men do not need to be seen. We do not want the world to praise as once visible useless for future missions, but mainly as we want the people to feel they did it.

As often as we all like to say we do a lot for charity, but don't want to talk about it, and yet we all want the world to know. Invisible Men and Women just enjoy the thrill of knowing what others wonder.

My night with Marjorie and Giselle was memorable and the exact details remain with me and my two beautiful friends.

The next morning I woke and left to read the papers and find my next mission, but it will have to wait until certain Presidential wannabe has all the coverage preventing even a bomb attack in Mumbai pushed to page 32. I felt great and it was a joy to know that I had done it. Yes, Reader this journal is for all to know, but you still have no idea who I am. I remain the Invisible Man.

Plus, almost forgot, taxi driver got $5,000 reward and the picture of Karl Perkins was in every paper. I smiled as I had changed the picture to the aide for the President Elect.

12

6:30am. Exeter Airport and I arrive back. Literally left New York and flew back into sunny UK. Back to Blighty. Well a slight drizzle in Exeter, but the sun has just started to come out. No one saw me leave; just as no one saw me arrive. I am invisible again and need to do something.

I manage to get an Air BnB with a couple in Exwick, Gary and Beverley. Lovely couple, lovely house, and just totally relaxed atmosphere. I arrived as agreed at 8:30, just as Gary leaves for Tiverton to work on his recycling route.

I make my way upstairs to a small single room and literally fall into a really comfy single bed. I am a little more than jet lagged as the evening before I was partying with Marjorie and Giselle. I also look to see I need to find work, cash is low and the American mission was expensive, but the thought of not going and have that evil cancer, with his hideous wig and misogynistic family in power at the White House meant my new found poverty all worth while, well acceptable.

I sleep for a few hours and realise it is three in the afternoon. I don't know about you reader, but it is always disorientating waking up from a deep sleep, thinking you have just closed your eyes for ten minutes to then find out you have been out, sparko, for seven hours.

The house is empty. Lovely note from Beverley saying to help myself to tea or coffee or fruit or cereals..... I use Air BnB often on travels under a few pseudonyms ranging from country to country. Today I am Andy. I make a cup of tea in a Disney Princess mug; more smiles. Three teaspoons of sugar as I love a cup of hot sweet tea.

I remember being in Moscow the day that Yeltsin stormed the parliament building in tanks. It was all a huge publicity stunt more than anything else. But I was there on a mission. More scary than the rednecks as placed myself in danger where there was no real escape. In the parliament building was a dissident poet that they were really after and I wanted to try to get him out. They were meant to storm the day after, but Yeltsin could not wait to parade round as the big man. In fact I had managed to gain access as his British propaganda agent to leak story of his arrival. Without question all bought the story, as it was too daft to not be true.

I had instigated a peaceful coup to help me make my escape with the poet. As I was having him released into my charge I found forty-three other political prisoners. Not sure how to get them out suddenly the tanks fired and in the panic I yelled to the guard "Quick, get them out, there is not meant for anyone to be here, Yeltsin will be furious!"

So there I am half an hour later with forty-four dissidents in my hotel room and as we sit round the corner from the parliament the dissident poet says that he missed his hot sweet tea. I smile and we drank hot sweet tea together. At that point I am hooked. Obviously not naming the dissidents saved and managed to get to Germany as travelling circus as the Kremlin thinks they all died in the takeover. The guard must of realised his mistake and declared all were dead and he would take care of bodies, and again feeling self satisfied with themselves the powers that be never bothered to check

80

his story. How do I know this? The guard now runs the circus for us.

So this Reader is why I need you to keep this journal safe as the Russians think they are all dead killed as planned in peaceful attack. The truth of the coup was a diversion to take focus away from the secret police executing forty-four political prisoners held in the cells below. I actually walked them out as cleaners before the cells were checked and cleared of staff, just before the tank 'accidentally' fired into the area. Working with another Russian Invisible Man we had forty-four from a morgue placed in the cells, dressed as cleaners initially, we had posed as part of the body bag team to clear dead bodies up to get us in, and the Russians so pleased with themselves that they had so successfully carried out their brilliant master plan nobody actually checked the bodies.

I smile to myself as we all crossed the border dressed as clowns and had clown ID that we joked was part of the act and the guards not wanting to be part of a joke just moved us on. One escapee was a billionaire oil tycoon who refused to sell his company to a Russian official. Funny thing is that Russian official became one of Russia's leaders and had to sell his stolen company to the Russian government in order to succeed to power; unknowing I was Russian Official that he sold it through and bought using the billionaire's money to seal the deal for literally 1% of it's worth. The same billionaire I helped escape used money he stole from Russian government bank account to buy back his company. As the government changed within six months and ex-heads were disappearing no one was any the wiser and he now works with the current Russian government from his base in the West. How funny life is as his nephew bought an English Football Club and they enjoy a lifestyle we all dream of, and they took care of their forty-three fellow escapees.

I went to see their team play my beloved West Ham United. A game we West Ham Fans claim as a victory as we won one all, well a draw was a win for us at the time. True West Ham fans always say that we will be in Europe next year (European Cup) if there's a war. I saw the two in the director's seating and sent a text from a mobile of a fan next to me and then erased. I watched as the text arrived and a huge smile came on his face. Half time came and the large TV screen had a message come up to a huge cheer from our fans. It read ' I cannot see you, but I hear you my West Ham Fan. Welcome always from your rivals Chairman'. He stood and was applauded by the whole ground. I had a small mirror in my pocket and let if catch the sun to shine. I could see him smile from where I was as he saw it flash.

This was a huge moment as the rivalry of a football derby have always been intense, but this one gesture resulted in all the fans cheering together and as the teams came out for the second half the West Ham team went to the home fans and applauded them as they in return we were applauded by their rival teams fans as well as players. It was quite emotional. The two chairmen stood side by side raised their hands together holding aloft and showing respect and pride, but mostly a shared love of this sacred game.

This became the main news story, front page and back, and the Russians nephew was interviewed, then looked to camera and said to my total disbelief and pride,

"We watched a magnificent game with sixty thousand fans, our friends who love the sport. I just wanted to say to a man, man to man, alongside all the Invisible Men we never know, and say that at that moment we never forget how easy it is to deploy peace."

Needless to say it was an amazing moment for the sport as fans exited, cheering together and the banter was hilarious; each giving as good as they got. There was no trouble, no police incidents and all the press remarked on what an amazing moment it was. Well not all, actually the paper we all love an know as just right of Attila the Hun, The Daily Mail led with scathing attack on Russian Billionaires Wealth and some story they had mocked up. Seems my Russian friends are not Tory enough for the Daily Mail.

Sorry for all the ramblings Reader, but if you ever come to the UK never buy this odious little rag. It paints a picture that would depress a clown of how the world is through their bitter, racist eyes, who have the inability to smile.

I remember the Prime Minister, right wing Tory, just the type of reader for the Daily Mail, was caught lying for the umpteenth time to the British public and they wrote an article on the story as if the man was a saint. We, as Invisible Men and Women knew the spoon-faced liar was hiding ill-gotten wealth in tax havens in Panama to avoid paying tax years ago. In fact one of my colleagues managed to get the evidence out. He cracked the computer database, risked his life as these accounts also Mafia and such clientele, to see the PM of Great Britain happy, knowingly placing his money with gangsters, drug lords and such people who run sex-slave operations to avoid paying tax.

I was gobsmacked when the same spoon faced liar hauled a comedian over the coals for using a tax loop and who asked about his crooked friends went on air to say it was not his place to comment on how others finances are run.

Sorry to rant Reader, but his journal can become a place to rant and a release for me, but it will never change my hatred of how the wealthy rule the poor and feel they are above the law feeling they should remain unchallenged themselves. Another reason my Reader to keep this journal safe as want to protect all Invisible Men.

I leave the house in Exwick and head to the Boston Tea Party, a wonderful coffee and healthy lunch spot in Exeter just down from one of the college's buildings. This is where I come to write my journal when in Exeter as they have a great poached eggs on toast and wonderful coffee. I enjoy my chats with great staff, Leon and his amazing beard and special moustache that his two girls love to pull on when he is at home being dad not running the cafe, Sophie, who I saw sing her own songs in the wonderful big space upstairs there, a real gem and a great night, is there smiling always, as are the beautiful Emma and Mandy whom I have got to know by name. Mandy has great hair.

I am now refreshed and content so good time to find work and on the street I meet a young man in his twenties called Tom who asks if I would like work. Now this turns out to be a pivotal moment for me as I see a new side to life.

Tom is the RFM (Regional Fund Manager) for a Home Fundraising Company. They employ and train people to go out knock doors and find members of the public to sign up for different charities.

Now I like most of us Reader think how annoying it is when these people knock on our door, but these people are just a phenomenal group of individuals. We have a picture we have built up from a negative assumption based on articles written in negative newspapers like the Daily Mail, and miss the fact that they raise millions for charity.

I pop into their office in the main high street and after what was the shortest of training sessions find myself a day later knocking doors in Plymouth. Knowing Tom alone has raised over two hundred and fifty thousand for charity, his deputy, bald, tall, funny, powerful presence from Northern Ireland is taking me out with a group of others. The job hires many who would seem unemployable, but they are incredible when they have the chance. I reflect on how many in our societies are overlooked without even being given a chance, but here Tom is like an inspiration. Tom was once homeless and needed a job, did this, was really good and a few years later running the place. There is a mixture of university students looking for part time work and young tearaways aged 19, to me.

The atmosphere is relaxed and we are then taught about the charity we will be championing and how it needs help. It is cancer charity and the mere fact 889 people a day are diagnosed with cancer is mind blowing enough. To then find one in four are left isolated and alone to face this life affecting silent killer makes me even more determined to do well. I then find out that the spoon faced liars government did not give out £234.4 Million in benefits as sufferers never asked for it, they never even knew they could claim as the anxiety and stress of coping is enough to deal with, makes me even more determined to make sure people know what they are entitled to and that they can help others.

I am on a train feeling that I cannot wait to make a difference. I know it will not be easy, as this government has enforced an austerity program on the poor that even Himmler and Goebbels could not sell to the people. Money is tight for everyone and I soon find those that have little give and those that could easily afford £3 per week say they cannot.

Now Reader, I am not anti-conservative as their values were always to responsibly help the poor without jeopardising the wealthy, but in recent years they see the money to help people should be made available to themselves and friends on other needless activities.

I remember braking the news of when the government sold off the Royal Mail that one man made over £37,000,000 on the deal as the share price was fixed at the wrong level. Of course the man in question was only the best man at the wedding for our Chancellor of the Exchequer!

Walking around town I saw the Exeter folk going about their business feeling that the Plymouth folk too would be easy going and chatty.

I spot a beautiful young woman with two children. She is from Guadeloupe, tall, elegant and seems to be struggling with her bags. I go to offer help. She is French speaking, but her English sounds sexy. I smile, as does she. She is a single mum from an abusive relationship who was left homeless as the father of her children just walked off and never paid the rents, leaving her with crippling debts. Luckily, the council stepped in to offer temporary accommodation and as she and the two charming girls get on the bus I wish them well. I notice how there are not many black people in the West Country and there is an air of casual racism about the people's attitude to minorities. A shame as the people here are not backward, just closed in due to lack of worldliness.

I remember seeing in New York a sign someone had painted on a wall by some moron from the rally saying. 'Blacks Out!' The sign was made totally inoffensive by a far more intelligent black person had written underneath, 'But he will be back soon.'

Walking back to my room after a day and night for the charity door sales I reflect on what will be my next mission.

I lie in bed wide awake thinking of all that had happened as after brief training I was introduced to James and literally in the streets of Plymouth door to door knocking. I remember a nineteen-year-old local lad, Jacob, who had been working a week already being full of energy. He got three people to sign that night and was called a charity hero. Jacob is an inspiring character as in the face of major adversity to many he has overcome and copes with the day-to-day pressure of life brilliantly. Then there was Andrew, a university student from Kent and larger than life Kyrstof from Manchester aged twenty. Again, a character with an incredible background where this job has given him a home and helped shape his future.

I could list everyone I met as they were all exceptional. Sam, a team leader who is a vegan and just really supportive to all, grounded and really nice to everyone. There were many students, red head Theo, such a great lad with a superb sense of humour. Dudzilla, another team leader who loves hugging people who would literally sign up more than anyone else, the lovely Norwegian student at Uni called V as no one could properly pronounce her name, Greta, a beautiful Italian student who also had a first day with me and a mature lady called Naomi who also started same day. There is a lot of transitional movement in the job as it is not easy or not as we are sold the job in the training.

Another larger than life character is Fabian. He makes an initial impression when you get him as he loves his music and you cannot but like him.

They say they pay for travel to work, which is sort of true, but not as this is a real bugbear for all that work there, everyone feels ripped off, but the company deals with a lot of lowest common denominator people as well so they put up with the situation. We had all arrived to the office, this is not paid, the two hours to get to site is; train fare only, but not your time travelling. It is a con, but I was grateful for work.

I remember the first door I knock as it opens I manage to say, 'Hi I am Andy and I am..' the door slams in my face and the occupier tells me to 'Go forth and multiply', but not exactly in those words. I smile and walk to the next door and see James watching. I look to him and still grinning say, "He said he'd rather not." James laughs and continues with his spiel on the doorstep of another house. Greta is on the doorstep of an elderly gentleman for ages and it seems he could sign up, but turns out he was enjoying the company. May be this is a job better suited to attractive young ladies, but then the door opens and a middle aged woman answers and proceeds to flirt outrageously with me. I think that she is going to sign. It is just £2.50 a week; yes that is all we ask, but most say they cannot afford it. Only £2.50 a week and it can make such a difference for the charity. But then without warning she shuts the door. I realise the talk of many sign ups in a day are true, but the goalposts have changed now.

Now, we cannot take less than £10 per month, back when high scores hit it was £5 per month. Plus you only had to be 18 before, but now no one under 21. The other thing I realised was these streets had been farmed for over fifteen years and the finding new donors was hard. But relentlessly this army of many backgrounds marches on and I am humbled by their attitude to do well and passion for the job.

If you ever go to Plymouth the streets are all built on steep hills. My feet ache at the end of the shift and it rained and we were freezing then rushing in taxi's back to the train station and home on another long train journey without pay. The atmosphere is good and all are in great spirits.

I reflect on the stories each tells and realise that if I had not done this job I would of probably been indifferent to the charity caller on my door, been suspicious of giving out bank details to a stranger, a little bit untrusting of the caller on my doorstep as they were not my social network, my usual group of friends, yet everyone endeared me with their passion and humour whilst being constantly often abused and insulted.

My faith in the human race had been restored working with these guys who have a thirty minute break at 5:30pm, which is not paid, and had to sit in the rain to have whatever food they could find to buy in some awful convenience store to hand. After which three hours more knocking of door ensued. I find it funny how after the trails of New York and the complexities of the mission just carried out, just how difficult this door to door knocking was, frightened of letting people down, passionate about the charity, hoping all the money reaches the charity we raise as this also was on my mind, and even though feeling like a fish out of water, actually I was a fish in water as it was thundering down on us, I had managed to get two sign ups.

I start to come back into the throng of the conversation on the train and come to realise that I am among an army of invisible people. They go through the streets up and down the country knocking doors, hoping for a second to be heard so that they can make a difference to their charity, make a sign up then they disappear into the night without even a thank you. The reward was knowing that their efforts would help thousands of sufferers going through the hardest time of their lives as a faceless champion without recognition.

My pride and admiration for those 'Peter Pan' like lost boys and girls grows and I manage to carry on knocking throughout that night with restored faith in people, marching from door to door, feeling I can only do my best and I can repay the faith they have placed in me letting them join them.

I slept well that night.

14

Reflecting on the past nights work in the morning I was tired and happy and surprised myself as I had signed up two people. It is hard to describe, but the exhilaration of signing up someone, knowing that the money would help someone's life become better for having the help it would bring was immense. I then reflect on how it is an awful shame that charities have to go cap in hand to the public and just how corrupt and despicable governments are in their total lack of true support.

I am told that if the public give a direct debit donation then 98% goes to the charity and we also get 25% gift aid from the chancellor's back pocket. But, if you drop a few pounds in a collection box 35% is taxable by the government. I soon learn that charity shops are not making money, but just about paying rents and that they are a way of keeping the charity in the publics eye as TV commercials are just too expensive. This made the work done by the home fundraiser seem even greater.

Oh yes, sorry Reader there is no chapter 13. Not superstitious, but not there for those that are.

Reflecting on the thoughts of how poor governments are squandering money, not helping people unless it seems they are helping themselves, happily letting charities struggle and not supporting in a way we all feel they should, I look for a local mission as want to stay 'smashing doors' as it is affectionately known.

Within a few seconds reading local paper I find something all Invisible Men and Women hate, corrupt councils. Now it may seem small amounts, but these grow and those that perpetrate this sort of robbery on a local level often rise to national level, become MPs and go on to extort greater theft and misuse of funds where the collateral damage is much higher.

Visiting a small Devonshire town I find just such a group. Small in size, but no lesser in statue of crooks and legal wrong doing. I say legal as they spend without conscience, but wrong morally as there are no watchmen to make sure they are stopped. Everything happens behind closed doors and even the public records are hard to decipher. This is why local government is home to some of the biggest crooks we produce.

Again happens to be a huge Tory belt Devon, but then again politics if often hereditary even today. My own mother would have voted for a member of the Gestapo had they worn a blue rosette. It is therefore that the West Country is easily fooled by those pandering to their need to make them feel middle class, installing fear that a vote to labour would mean everyone on benefits being given better housing than them and building divides and creating greater poverty gaps, is stock and trade in today's political arena. Say whatever needs to be said and any opposition met place the fear of God into them to dare use their brains and think differently. So I stroll through a town where everyone is struggling, mainly to keep up with the Jones's as they say, full of their own importance by being a 'friend' of someone on the council or their self elected Mayors. Yes reader you do not have to look further than your local councilors to find corruption of money destined for the public backing projects that are supporting a few related to those that are administering the wealth. On hearing one story I feel I must as an Invisible Man investigate.

I am on the train back after another full on door-to-door knocking session and chatting to James, fellow fundraiser and heavy metal rocker and philosopher. A really fascinating guy. I am enthralled listening to him. He is so wise on so many levels and then discovers he has returned to society after taking a year out living like a monk in isolation. He was working fundraising as he was getting back into society mind frame and we chatted about meditation and how James can literally deflect all his stress away from inwardly going to his own quiet place in the middle of a chaotic train and I watch wishing I could. He tells me I could, but I know I would never be able to switch off my brain long enough to get there; wherever there is.

Jacob is bouncing around the train as he has a personal best of sign ups. We all revel in his joy and think on how he has helped someone he will never meet and given someone else hope.

The days melt one into another and I continue as a fundraiser. It is hard and the people I work with amazing. I am saddened each day as those with little struggle to give and the majority of Devon with nice cars and houses refuse to even try to help another. They even refuse to spend 30p a day on helping another rather than spending ten times that on filling up their big petrol guzzling cars. It is often all about status in the Tory middle classes and nothing of substance. The poor they are also trying to be middle class, but most of the donations come from those truly hard up.

I wonder how these self interested, sad people became so untrusting and afraid to help anyone other than themselves. Many lie to say they are already giving, yet obviously they are not. The lies and stupidity gives this away. But even those on the poverty line often take out their frustration on the charity fundraiser unaware of what is happening on the other side of the door.

I was in Plymouth once again and knocked a door that seemed quiet and inoffensive. It was dark out and about 8:30pm so this was not always a wanted knock from the other side. As I knock as if in tandem a huge row erupts the other side of the door. I stand my ground as I was there as the charity's champion and if I ran away then I would be no better than those that shout abuse.

The door opens and a middle-aged woman answers and without warning throws a mid-size Labrador at me. I catch this beautiful dog in mid air and for a few seconds this dog and I stare at each other. The dog presumably was laying in front of the fire one minute then in my arms the next in the cold. He looked as confused as I. Without a moments hesitation therein I start my pitch. The woman looks me up and down then screams for me to 'F' off and take the 'F'ing dog!' A guy appears as she walks back into the house. Hen pecked look on his face he looks to me confused as I stand there holding the dog. A few seconds pass before he thinks I have come to steal his dog. I explain who I am, what I think just happened and they are having a row over the dog. I happily return the dog that the man obviously loves and say that possibly this is not a good time, but would he be interested in supporting the charity. He also says that he would rather not.......

I watch the door shut and as if in another universe I am back in the street and it is freezing. This occurrence in one form or another happens every night, day after day, but the exhilaration of having that one good person sign up made it all worthwhile. I can think of easier work, but there is nothing to rival the adrenaline rush of having truly made a difference.

You see Reader, if you shut the door on this strange bunch of incredible individuals, a sort of army of invisibles as you will often never see them again, then you are shutting the door on the people they represent that need your help more than ever. Often we are afraid to trust the unknown and feel that anyone on your doorstep is only there to con you.

Take it from me that you should at least listen, see that they have ID that can be verified, and know that we can all afford to donate at least £10 per month. I respect we all have the right to say no just as much as we have the right to say yes, but do note that if the individual on the doorstep is from Home Fundraising then the money you donate will go to the charity. This is no smaller mission carried out by fundraisers across the country than the work of the Invisible Man.

Time to get back to my new mission.

15

Now Reader I want to help you to look beyond the press and follow up on what you were promised next to the reality; you will be amazed at the amount of corruption at local political levels there is. Often small fiddles build and the perpetrators become bolder, more self-assured that they are above the law, too clever to be caught and soon millions is misused and lost. From small deceptions come bigger lies and then all is cultivates is more hardship for the people.

So what is my mission? Who is the Target? No surprise I guess a councilor who as a Mayor saw an opportunity for a substantial payday.

A few years ago a TV show was hosted by a lady called Mary Portas. She is a wonderful woman looking to help struggling towns revitalise themselves and increase footfall. All worked whilst the TV cameras were there, but once that circus had left town so did the people's positive attitude towards Mary and what she was trying to achieve. But Mary battled on and managed to get £6,000,000 to be given to towns to help them pay to help themselves. Sadly, the local councilors saw that if they headed up the groups they would be able to control where the money went. Well this Mayor headed a committee that was awarded £100,000 and seems no one monitors the spend or reactions as over the past year the townsfolk were up in arms at the stupidity of the group and wasted money spent.

So it just so happens as in Devon, a Tory council gets £100,000 and a group of excited councilors look to spend on their pet projects and increase their spend by match funding with more tax payers money awarded by themselves to themselves. An award from a Conservative Government went unchallenged and it is announced a new Portas Group for the town.

So a year on what have they achieved to date? Nothing to write home about. In fact footfall has not increased at all and money has been spent, but as I remarked once that upon looking at the group in charge they all dress better than before. What have they done with the money?

From a shop in town given by the council for free to advertise with and use as a base I read and passing by townsfolk look to remark what a waste of time. Most derisory remarks are followed by laughter and tutting of heads, but I discover by complete accident that these wonderful locals were completely unaware of a cunning master plan about to unfold.

The people were furious about a fibreglass gorilla bought to be placed in the high street for a prickly sum that subsequently cost a fortune to repaint twice after vandalism and having costly CCTV put in to monitor the beast 24/7. Look closer and you will soon unearth the subterfuge and corruption lurking underneath. The artist and gorilla are legitimate, but the repaint by local artist was suspect. You see no one knows who vandalised the gorilla or in fact if it had been. Just one morning new artist, one of committee from Portas Group, sat painting the gorilla. No one knew anything and nothing was investigated, and this is a pattern used that often goes un-missed. The use of Chinese whispers in small communities is the way most cons are worked. I found that the artist who repainted the gorilla after the vandalisation was having a meeting with the ex-mayor before the incident a week before, setting in place plans for such an occurrence and costs for works should it ever be deemed necessary. It may also come as no surprise that the company paid to install the CCTV were also connected to the group and new ex-mayor. The thing is Reader, unless you look hard you just see local press manipulated with misinformation and the youth are to blame.

I am back in Exmouth on a break after a two-hour door knocking session having people of all ages, sizes, nations and religious denominations tell me to go forth and multiply to me and my motley crew of fundraisers. Many self-important council type bods and I reflect on the Portas group again. I think of how with me is an army of good hearts looking to find help for our charity helping those that truly need help. I listen to the wonderful way all keep their spirits up and the laughter and think how much good that £100,000 would have done the charity. Jacob, aged 19, is now in charge as a team leader. I am amazed how this job has galvanised an angry young boy into a committed, focused young man. He is there inspiring his team and looking forward to help us all get sign ups we need to sustain our presence. Because we are fund raisers and as such have to raise funds or why are we even out on the streets?

We walk miles, knock one hundred and fifty doors a day each and as the hour strikes nine we have to stop by law and we are ready to travel home. All are ecstatic as we managed to sustain a sign up total that exceeded our daily quota and look to see text to see if we were the top team. We were and beat Dudzilla, who consistently scores more than anyone. It is the end of the week and tonight we can celebrate that we have in simple terms helped not only the awareness of the charity to the public in a positive manner, but we have raised much needed funds for them to continue their great work. I look at the positive that this team has achieved and then as we ride the train home reflect on a weekend of more delving into how the Portas Group looking down on others has not done anything near as noble.

It is a beautiful morning and I walk into town as an Invisible Man looking to investigate this Portas Group further. Whenever the group is mentioned the name evokes disdain and total disinterest from the locals. I have taken a bus from Exeter to visit to see what has been happening. It is this total disinterest that the corrupt ex-mayor is looking for; she now is ready to make her move. I see a new poster go up listing all the amazing accomplishments that they have achieved.

Many were projects already in flow they latched onto and many had profits back, not seen, from stalls space sold. I laugh to see the omission of the internet radio set up they spent thousands on through another committee members electronics company buying that did not materialise, as they bought all the wrong equipment and argued over what could and could not be played. The whole point of Radio is it is a diverse medium that caters for a diverse public and not everyone will listen to everything.

Yes Reader, it seems that whenever sanctimonious councilors are left in charge or at the helm nothing ever gets done; lot of money spent on meetings to talk, but in the end the money runs out and all is soon forgotten as old newspaper pages fish and chips are sold in.

There was one day the Radio Station set up was working. Well it was two huge speakers in the street directing up and down the main high street connected to two CD decks and a microphone. There was a town day the group latched onto and in full military coup style took over. This gave the Portas Bods in charge time to stand around pointing out their great deeds and taking all the credit. As they all strut around like peacocks fun of their own importance I joking remark to one lady looking as if she wanted to shoot the lot of them, " Well at least since getting £100,000 they are all dressing better." She laughed with me.

The Radio idea was dying, as they were all concerned that they must not offend anyone and feared something offensive may be said over the airwaves and reflect on them. This meant they would never play Rap Music or anything they really knew nothing about. It had to be all about them, all for them. They would have no idea who Tupac was, but he was one of the most inspirational poets of the recent generation. A Shakespeare of his times.

So, to my amusement, that was not lost on others, a young teenage girl, who was a daughter of one of the committee is given the task of being DJ. With the speakers on full blast she watches proceedings and remarks, "Oi, look at those spastics over there!" and laughs out loud. Sat watching beside her was special needs children and people enjoying the day. I almost fell off the bench I was sat on. Not one of the Portas Group felt there was a problem with what she said, and much worse followed, but one rapper played, and the thought that he would of been black was enough to make them shut the station down.

It is not just in local towns, but I spoke to locals in Exeter about their local Radio Station that now goes out on FM. Many laughed and said they never listen as shows are just so boring and all started getting annoyed as they were never listened to when they complained. Apparently one DJ would continually say the most offensive, racist remarks, but even with public outcry continues unashamedly on air and it seems casual racism is accepted in Devon. Numbers have fallen greatly and yet as it is council run no one seems to care as long as it turns on and off as publicised; and paid for by the tax payers money.

This was the day, the fateful day that the town launched its new town logo. It was a triumph for the Portas Group as it was they that had bought all this about. A new sign to bring together the people and increase footfall. Yes Reader, I cannot see myself the point in this, but bear with me as now the Invisible Man steps up to try to end this corruption.

Rumour was that the ex-Mayor had put twenty thousand pounds of their own money into this logo. Previously complaining how when the sign was initially turned down by the labour council it had nearly bankrupted them. Well it got its day as it was to be unveiled by the Portas Group later that day in front of the whole town; well about a hundred as most of the footfall had not bothered attending as knew day would be lackluster. The whole day accumulated in an evening outdoor feast that only a few could afford and of course all the Portas Group got it for free. They are the only ones really attending except a few members of groups hoping to get in with a chance of money from the £100,000 they reside over.

The sign was unveiled in their shop window as the new jewel in their crown. A podium outside and all the Group there on the podium in designer outfits bought for the occasion as press would be there, with money given to each from the fund, looking smug and holier than thou. Reader I do love these moments.

A small crowd gathered and I manage to stand just behind the man from the local newspaper. I knew this editor of the paper and by standing behind him kept my invisibility as well as stage whispering my journalist into the right questions. He of course was not in on the ploy, but knew him as a real hack wanting to make the big time, but only ever putting negative spins on articles as a lover of sensationalism. Again all is slotting nicely into place.

Often reader we look back at moments where we say that we wished we had only done this or only done that after the event. An Invisible Person does it at the time. They risk exposure. They risk personal attack. They know this is the only way for the public to see the Emperor's New Clothes or in this Portas Group the Emperor's New Designer Clothes.

Prior to this announcement I had wandered casually watching the day and in particular bumping into this very reporter I stand behind right now. Each time I had a different hat or was looking as with my wife and child or made him over hear a conversation. Subliminally I had primed this awful hack to be my Weapon of Mass Destruction. His previous writings of attending other perfectly normal events and placing a twist on it in the most negative manner, disregarding any positivity or good light to shine, this Uriah Heep of a journalist was already primed to bring the day down to one seedy moment. I was just there to make sure he got the right point of view for his article.

Reader, often dealing with journalists like this, an editor of a worthless rag, a man of no integrity, who loves to highlight others misfortune so not to have to reflect on his own miserable life. These failed individuals are the greatest tools to use when you are an Invisible Person.

I had fed him information all day and it had not taken long for him to grow with excitement as he saw a huge breaking story that he could possibly be lead reporter on national TV with. Oh, yes Reader, I also gave him that last thought too.

The moment arrives and a speech about the painting, the sign being a new beacon to bring people to the town was unveiled and all stood on stage looking smug and self satisfied with themselves. They had done it. Each had money for the outfits, money for their night eating paid for on the main table, on stage being praised for the work they have done, pocketing large amounts of cash legitimately without anyone the wiser to themselves, and feeling that there is no one smart enough to ever catch them or their brilliance out. The look on their faces about to be seen was literally going to be priceless.

I saw the same gleam flash across my reporter's eyes as I had seen as I pumped him with the information. He thought he had pieced everything together from various clues, but never realised all came from me. I could see him getting nervous and for a second thought he was going to bail on account of being too nervous, but then I whispered in a soft voice, as if I was Obi-Wan Kenobi telling him to feel the force, 'Think of BBC news at Ten, lead anchor.'

Within seconds his hand is raised and the crowd turn. The ex-Mayor feeling proud with grin from ear to ear looks as if to say 'Yes?'

As everyone looks in silence he asks,

"How much did the logo cost?"

Immediately my target is flustered and her smile evaporates as she tries to avoid answering with statements in panic mode like,

"How can you put a price on a town's identity?" and, "It is priceless, treasure to live forever."

But I am egging on my dimwit and again he asks, "True, so what did it cost?" I cry out a mumbled, "Answer the Question." The crowd sense blood and many in the crowd see the gorilla behind them that fuels only the kind of anger a person scorned can be induced. Others shout out, "Answer the question," followed by, "Let's hope not as much as the gorilla," and all laugh.

A few of the committee have started to back off the stage, as they are feeling more than a little uncomfortable.

"Oi, where you lot running to?" I shout.

The crowd sense blood and I see my moron editor getting excited so I steer him into his next piece.

"Why not tell me now of how much?" he shouts as I whisper the words behind him.

One of the group on stage panics, "Thirty Thousand Pounds! "

The whole crowd go silent and then look at the ex-Mayor who trying to compose herself and looking daggers at her colleague then tries to justify the expense as my friend in front of me stands writing it all down. He seems too thick to see the real story he already has in his head, I spent a day in the most boring event ever making sure he got it and now he lets go! I have to say that the explanation is not bad and although hostile crowd not happy they seem to accept that there is nothing to be done.

I whisper once more in my dimwitted friend's ear.

"But was this not a sign you as the Head of Portas had stated previously before the Portas money that you have paid for and gifted to the town? " He says and sees he is in charge and continues with me prompting from behind.

"So why has it cost anything? And who is the designer? Who will be given the contract to print all the signs and new welcome boards as people drive into town? "

The crowd looks confused and then at the Journalist that they had once held in low esteem and then back to the group stuck on stage.

I see my man writing as if the penny has finally dropped. He turns to look behind at me, but I have already gone.

A week later I am sat in coffee shop reading my duped journalist's article, which did see him interviewed for fifteen seconds on BBC SouthWest, in the local paper. A major investigation had discovered that the Head of the group took £30,000 and paid £5,000 to her brother-in-law to do the design. A further £25,000 contract went to another committee member who literally set up a company to handle making the signs. All the committee has £1,000 clothing allowance, which was on display that day and the gorilla was made by another committee member and repainted by another and the CCTV surveillance was a contract given to another committee member. All would come out later in even more acrimonious fashion as each were appalled they were not able to steal as much as the others. Sadly, there will be no prosecutions, but the group have disbanded and new people in charge of a fund with no funds.

My dear Reader, please keep this journal safe and realise that corruption will always be present and we the people must be prepared to speak up at the right time to ask the right questions before it is too late.

Again I reiterate, Einstein once said something like, "Evil will always rule as long as good men stand by and do nothing," or something like that, and that is what we the Invisible People have as a code of practice.

16

So two missions, each different, but neither more nor less important than the other. But my time in Exeter is coming to an end. I saw an article in the Daily Mail that had caught my eye. Now as said before if ever there was a paper to avoid it is this fascist rag. When looking through the paper you have to read between the lines the Invisible Man can see a story so blatantly trying to cover and yet cover up at the same time, that I have to go and investigate. I am going to my favourite city in the world, London.

I sit here writing at the Boston Tea Party and chatting to stunning young girl called Beth, who first persuaded me to pop in for a coffee, and as usual relax and feel at home. Leon joins us and I enjoy a chat as Beth then leaves to tidy up and Elliot comes to take Leon away and then a series of smiles from Sophie, Emma and all staff make me feel there is a reason to carry on. I hear a cup smash and see the lovely Mandy tell someone it's OK.

The night before I leave for London I have a moment with my home fundraising friends. My time there was brief and proud to of been part of the team, but yet remained invisible, or so I thought. Seems I was involved in helping the guys and girls out more than I had realised as I gave them each advice as to what I would do in the situations they presented me with.

There have been so many amazing characters that it was easy to move within unnoticed. I say goodbye to Jacob, so proud of the person he has become, Dudley, Dudzilla, the man with more heart than most whose hugs lift everyone at the office. Jethro, who works for his church and tirelessly as a fundraiser and a really wonderful guy. James my Rock God who is such a gentle soul. Theo the Red, quite literally nuts and so intelligent. Olya, the Russian brains and beauty. Lizz always wanting to be seen. Ash, a quiet man, the silver fox who stresses over things that do not matter, as he is truly loved by all. James the Beast as he likes to be known, who behind all the bluff and bravado is a really kind big hearted person. Luke K and Luke R both wonderful individuals and Chris, who returned from youth work was just a solid human being and such a positive person. Callum, who was always wanting to achieve more than he thought he could, yet when he relaxed achieved to promotion and saw his way forward. Callum was pure and honest, no malice and hope he gets into IT. So many to mention, but also not to forget Tom, the twenty-seven year old boss of the region. A solid young man I will always admire and his passion and enthusiasm will always inspire. Even those that he had to fire will always respect him. My only fear is he becomes too much company man and looses sight of himself as he objection handles anyone telling him something he knows company does not want to listen to, but built in to him is the desire to win the argument. All the fundraisers will be missed, all Invisible heroes many will never meet, but they will of changed many peoples' lives.

As I leave I see new team leader whom I had a real pleasure of working my last day with, Ryan. Old school young man that has a real passion for life, for the job raising funds and feel one day he will be running a place himself as a born leader.

Ryan and I chat and he too is to leave as he works the summer at festivals and is enjoying living his life rather than living to work for someone else's life. I love the way he is so laid back and supports the ones he works with.

I stand outside the building in the sunshine and Jacob gives me a hug. Maria walks by who is a great girl and coming back now her exams are over. Theo stands outside with Jacob to have a cigarette and I smile as they campaign for cancer charities today. Theo the Red who asks cheekily if you want to taste his ginger nuts gives me his number to keep in touch and I am happy to do so. They have no idea of my other life as an invisible and I wish them all well and depart.

Sorry Reader, but want to say few words again about Tom as I will endeavor to help him find his dream of performing as a rapper one day.

Invisible Men do not only highlight the corrupt, we often highlight the individual that lifts us up. This young man inspires and gains the respect of all that encounter him. I can pontificate he raised personally quarter of a million for charity, and other accolades, but I feel that Tom is the epitome of all that we should celebrate as a society.

Three years ago, as stated Tom was homeless and needed a job. Found something he was quite brilliant at with Home Fundraising and soon rose quickly through the ranks to running a whole region, but this is not his most endearing attribute.

Tom is charity through and through. Not just raising vast amounts, but for the way in which he uses his position to help others is why he stands out. Tom wants to offer all the lost lads and lasses a chance to find a job and train them, to give them the same opportunity he had, and took, so that they can also find themselves a better life. I encountered Tom as a homeless man with a young daughter and he just took me in, trained me, was hard on me as well, but through him I learnt a lot.

I am twice his age and learnt so much and as an Invisible Man I hope he heard my talks with him that he must never loose sight of the man he was to become the company man; as the company man he became less, for him not thinking outside their rules the company would loose more than a great asset, and he needed to continue to see outside their blinkered world of how things are done.

17

In the world of Invisible we learn everyday that we do not know everything. That we all can learn from each other and that no one is better than another. Just sometimes others can do things better than you, but you will always have something you can offer to enhance their world. Never sell yourself short.

I have left the teams behind and find myself in Exeter library having a coffee. I see they have a share a coffee jar instead of a tip jar. Money collected goes towards buying those that cannot afford a drink or bite to eat something. I ask the happiest staff in town and they say they started it in December 2015. People have responded well by buying a coffee and throwing change in the pot. I sit and see a few tramps stay in the sun outside at the tables all drinking a coffee and having a piece of cake. The homeless come and get served, made to feel welcome and also make the community aware. I am truly bowled over.

I leave Exeter for London thinking well done Devon, a few let the area down, but the majority of you left positive reflection against the sea of negativity from those that should do better. So many that would not give to charity for their own greed would not allow it to those that so generously give day in day out, I thank you all for a balanced look at society and overall faith in us as human beings restored.

I pack my little car and fill up with petrol and as I turn the key to start the engine I smile as I feel I am leaving a place where hope survives. I leave behind an army of

Invisible people making sure the world is a better place for millions of people that will benefit from what they do.

I drive along out of the service station off to the M5 I smile as I love my little car and soon am laughing as an old tramp mooning at the passing traffic - reality check - off I drive.

As the music plays in the car I keep reflecting about how unjustly those fundraisers are distrusted and found other local based charities had resorted to dirty tactics and once again the misplaced distrust, who listened to fabricated stories of the charity not receiving the money to other fables retold as if gospel like Chinese whispers and each an exaggerated untruth.

I write this again Reader as feel we should all question what we hear more and look deeper into who is saying what. I ask you Reader to answer to yourself as to how many times have you been party to a story or a slur, unwittingly trusted it was true, yet found out later it was a negative posting of a jealous, disenfranchised friend. Too often is probably the honest answer. Never? Well then guess you have been living in a bubble or you were the first to throw the stone. I admit I used to be guilty of not questioning. A negative is often used to displace the truth to hide the real story. Whether it came from jealousy or just trying to undermine someone else for his or her own gain. We look closer and find that this ploy is used to deflect anyone from truly looking at what is not being said.

They say the first ten minutes of driving you concentrate and the rest of the time you are on autopilot. Well without realising I have arrived at my friends in Croydon. I love London, but Croydon is the most toxic part of anywhere I have ever been.

You see this new mission is not just one individual, but a whole group who use the press and their lofty platforms to confuse and steel from all around. Indiscriminately, without conscience. Yes once again we hit the politicians Reader, for they have come to our attention again. An army of individuals collectively as well without integrity or morals this band of thieves whose mission of self-importance without care or compassion, certainly no integrity, they mame, injure or destroy all that get in their way. These are the career politicians looking to benefit only one thing in their seedy rise to power, themselves.

Now to the Invisible these are not easy prey to bring down, even though my last subjects have helped me immensely through their greed and stupidity. The career politician is a completely difference animal. They deflect the blame and rise more derision on less powerful groups to hide their own disgraceful objectives.

Recently campaigns to have the UK leave Europe have been sidelined to racist nonsense of more Romanians than live in Romania flooding into the UK. These dangerous, evil entities use others causes to stand on the backs of to rise to power or if the cause fails to stomp down on the one below.

Now Reader do not think I am going to expose a Tory MP having an affair with a stripper or using tax payers money to buy boys, that would be too easy. This is more than a junior minister selling information for cash. No I

114

have watched the rise of complete idiots through the ranks of government. Objectionable and offensive men who baffle all that they remain in office. But word is of a secret dossier that exists that at present in the wrong hands keeps this people safe.

One offender has recently had a run in with Junior doctors and lost the battle after having many quit due to his stupid policies and unfair handling of the situation and a minister that worked in education, that every teacher in the land called a moron who knows not what he is talking about, which was proved right, yet he still kept his job.

The government seemed to follow down the road of irresponsible policy after stupid, not thought out ideas, and yet the cabinet has within a body of people that would of been sacked from sweeping the warehouse floor for their inadequacies. There is also another power looking to surface after being the Mayor of this great city, whose lies and double dealing leads him to now pander to the masses to pave his way to becoming the next leader and Prime Minister. A hideous bully and over the next few months we will no doubt see extraordinary theft and misuse of public money when he ran City Hall. It seems he sold much of the wealthy property to find cash for his moronic schemes to his friends working in the city. The Olympic Village sold for peanuts to his mate and that of his fellow ministers in deals that lined his own pocket.

But I am not here to prove that as you only have to look into just a few of the names, do a small amount of research and hey presto the evidence is there to see. No I want to find the dossier and expose the creeps that work underneath the skin of those trying to do better. This underbelly of scum are my next target and far more dangerous than anything I have encountered so far as these are the calculating pariahs that build bombs where they have been to cover their tracks and allow others to take the blame.

But they are not fallible. They will make a mistake and the Invisible Man and Woman will be there to shine a light for all to see. For these all fall foul of thinking they are so clever, and they are, but a great American once said something along the lines of being able to fool some of the people some of the time etc etc etc.

Sat having a coffee in the centre of Croydon that had been burnt down during the riots and yet was such a shit hole no one even noticed I look around as recently investigating homelessness in the borough I was subjected to some of the most callous and indescribably thick people I have ever encountered.

Saying that must give credit where credit is due. At Croydon Job Centre I met and dealt with a man giant called Karl, who was the most charming and helpful man ever to meet in such an establishment who treated everyone with care and respect. His colleague Ian was similar and they did everything they could do to help a river flow of hopeless cases flowing in and out of the exchange. I sign on and it takes the team two weeks to be able to see me and then went to housing where the housing officer I saw should have been arrested as a criminal. She made us an appointment on Christmas Eve to discuss my daughter and mine's homelessness. Without a shred of interest we were processed and dismissed to live on the streets with no money and no place to live.

My main problem was I was teetotal, non-drug taking, never been in prison, honest guy with a sixteen year old daughter who wasn't pregnant. We just never fitted any of the criteria so they could know what to do with us.

But this is another story for another time, all to say is that Christmas being English and loving irony we worked Christmas day, Boxing Day and the days after as homeless people looking after the homeless with Crisis.

But the reason I say all this is we can all fall through the gap Reader. None of us are infallible. It is just listening to how the government show off on how they have an incredible record on benefit cheats and how they are getting more people into work and less homeless makes my blood boil. This is why I go after politicians myself in most cases as the lies they tell and the twisted figures they report with the aid of the press like the Daily Mail millions suffer needlessly. If they really did their job and acted responsibly and unafraid to make mistakes they would make huge strides to turning this country round. But they just focus on the negative and fear mongers whom to blame; for we love a scapegoat.

I read articles in the Mail about the number of benefit cheats stealing from the people. I think the amount of benefit fraud that actually happens from this on benefit, including those who took an extra week as they forgot to say when they started work, is about less than 2%. Yet read the papers it is about 80% on benefits are cheats and liars. Many are there for no fault of their own, just bad governments forcing businesses to close due to their inept policies, which again brings me to my target. Why are they still working when for most of the average public the horrendous mistakes they have made would of led to anyone else being sacked, but no these politicians carry on regardless.

18

It is eleven in the morning and sat in BAFTA, 195 Piccadilly, I have a coffee and collect my thoughts. Yes I am a member of BAFTA. Have been for years. It has changed so much in the past decade, sadly not for the better. The main staff are truly wonderful and all live up to the standards set by the amazing Terry Beurg, now this woman was the best front of house person I have ever met. She cared about everyone and they in return adored her.

The restaurant has a fun team of staff, but sadly the old BAFTA, which stands for British Academy of Film and Television Arts, and is now desperately trying to move members out so they can be this corporate event venue. A hideous team of an executive committee now organise things without members having any say. All of them not elected and seem to act like dictators without any accountability. Reader you must be thinking this is my next mission, but no. It is pointless as to try to show them up or change it will achieve nothing.

The one thing that does confuse me is BAFTA has charity status and yet operates like a blue chip company and there is nothing charitable about the prices they charge. There have been a dynamic duo in charge for far too long and all the members would like to literally kick them out of the building or club, as they like to refer it to. It seems they are highly corrupt and turned BAFTA from an Academy into loads of different gong shows. They have a BAFTA award for best use of a tin opener it seems. So many different awards and each growing less in significance.

As a member I get to vote. This is all fun and yet redundant as it seems whoever the members vote for the huge stars from America, that gave lack luster performances, but whose presence is demanded by the TV companies that buy the rights, always are nominated. Once a group of us wanted to see the percentages to see how the votes are counted and told it was secret and as such no one was allowed to see. Yes folks the BAFTA's as far as many are concerned are rigged, but who cares, it is not as if they make a difference to the world.

As an Invisible Man I have no real desire to bring the place down, at the moment, but it seems the charity commission has been investigating them and the team investigating were linked so it was rigged it seems and rumours fly around non-stop, but I fear if the two corrupt little Demigods are not removed by next year there will be a revolt there. I just wish they would resign and new blood bring back the word Academy to BAFTA as this was the intention from the founders many years ago.

Still, sat here having expensive coffee in a tiny mug, that is only a stone's throw from parliament and the seat of power, happy chappy.

Now to work out how and what I can do to get access to one of the most heavily guarded buildings in the world and then walk out with confidential files? This sounds like a daft question Reader, but what do you think you would do? No I really think if you stop reading and think of what you would do, you'll be amazed at how the daftest of ideas actually seems to be the most obvious. Think. What would you do?

Me, well at this moment in time and having had a couple of days to contemplate, my plan is to do what you are doing, if not right now, in a few minutes time. Put my journal down and think laterally. That is what I am going to do. Stop writing and think laterally, as well as take five minutes to visit the little boys room and then go for a walk.

See you shortly, and if you really think about it, some of your best ideas have come from sitting on the toilet have they not? We all use that time to off load more than, well to contemplate what we are doing once we finish, you know what I mean. Sorry got to dash need the loo.

19

Hi, I'm back and sadly nothing to report other than that was a load off my mind. Kept thinking of…. sorry this is getting nowhere. If sat on the loo doesn't work, go for a walk. I am off to walk down to Parliament and visit the site of my next mission.

As I pack my papers an attractive young girl arrives and asks if I am Dudley Ramsden, part of Arts Council as she needs to meet to discuss my meeting the select committee in Parliament. Blimey! I thought, that toilet was magical. I never said yes or no just shook her hand and said hi. Off we rush to a treasury meeting and in an office in Parliament.

She is a pretty girl, with long brown wild hair. Long and wavy and dead sexy. I guess even if she gets in trouble she'd give a look and all would be forgiven. Her name is Vesna, Croatian.

Just as we are leaving I run back up BAFTA stairs to say one second to Vesna and quickly Leave a message for Dudley Ramsden, "Hi, when Dudley Ramsden arrives please tell him the meeting has been cancelled and that we would call him in a couple of weeks. Parliament for you", I say as I hear them say, " Who shall we say….?"

" Vesna." I call out as disappearing and they think it is a man's name as why not, and Vesna thinks I am calling after her. She looks back and smiles and I think of Marjorie.

In seconds I am in a diplomatic car and being whisked to the treasury offices close to Parliament. Feeling not in my intended building, but we enter, I am given a badge and then whisked in a lift to basement and walk into Parliament underground. In no time at all I am Dudley Ramsden from the Arts Council and walk into a room where nobody knows me. All except one woman who is arriving later. I sit and open dossier and see we are discussing the Arts going forward for a budget proposal. It is a pet subject of mine so already feel energised. Just got to remember to be out before late woman arrives.

Minister stands and then in walks my target, the Secretary of State for Justice. He walks in as if he owns the place. His on screen persona does not do him justice and in the flesh this guy is an even bigger flesh crawling creep. He takes the folder from Vesna in his stride, throws it on the table and then sits and demands tea.
"How do you want it, with or without milk?" I say and stand to make. He is dumbstruck.

"I meant one of the servants to make." He replies with the civility of one of Dickens most malevolent characters. Being in the room with him is as pleasant as sat with a pernicious kind of bladder infection. Like some obsequious, cadaverous moneylender, he operates without a sign of any decency in any fibre of his body. This man is creepy to meet.

"So sorry, you just seemed to throw it out there as if we were all at your beck and call," I reply. There is a silence as I make my way to the tea and coffee. The lady serving tries not to laugh and smiles at me.

"I'm going to make myself one, anyone else?"

There is a silence and then Vesna chips in, " Well if you're making then I'll have an Earl Grey."

"It's OK sir, I'll do that for you," says the waitress come lady making drinks.

"Oh that's very kind of you," I reply and take my seat. I look down at the folder and see this creep who already has screwed over our education system was about to try to do with the Arts.

"Sorry, have we met?" enquires my minister.

"No, I think not." I reply, "but this is a dangerous dossier of destruction is it not?" I follow up with.

All at the table feel uncomfortable and I stand and walk about the room to deflect further attention as well as collect teas made and serve them.

"So here I read that you now want to take away all the funding for the Arts, except of course the Opera House, although severely cut, and blimey, whoever this little Arts group in Scotland, are they friends of anyone, the Queen's personal theatre group, well it spells a total explosion in the governments face if it is followed through."

"Sorry?" chips in the Minister for Death as I refer to him. An awful little career politician and one of my missions hits as he will murder any good cause for his own best interests.

"Well, folks, you bought me in as an advisor and I am saying this is stupidity at its highest level."

I look and smile at Vesna who conveys in one look that it is the brainchild of the Minister.

"But then again genius." I reply. I watch a totally confused table of the Minister and lackeys look to one another and then smile as the word genius brings them back on side.

"Whoever wrote this shows exactly what may be a good way to save money and yet reading between the lines it is obvious that the writer wants us to realise the ramifications of how many of us here in this room would loose their jobs if it went ahead."

Again, I see poor Vesna look worried, as obviously it was her idea the think tank to get me in, or whoever I was meant to be.

"The courage and the wisdom shown by this committee to tackle this daunting project reforms my faith in politicians, and, well, human nature."

All look around at each other smugly, except my hit that was now confused and worried as he had no idea who I was or what I was saying. Had I suggested that the dossier was to be implemented or not; or was I saying that the document they were to agree is merely a template to avoid? I started to realise I had control of the meeting, but as with all Invisible Missions realised that the hit had to lead.

I opened up discussion and asked who knew anyone at the Opera House? Of course my Arts hating MP, chairing the debate, knew someone as well as had contacts with the 'Scottish Group' who would be a shining light on Government's benevolence on small community projects. I show incredible enthusiasm at all my hit says and he seems to gain momentum and yet shows signs he is uncomfortable agreeing with his own report as I have made him feel as if to do so would be political suicide.

"What I am grateful to hear is how you sir," to my moron of a hit, "have courageously put together this dossier and looked at how it would be financially beneficial to all at the table and help save on government spending elsewhere as a template to try to achieve what is required and yet use to increase Arts spend."

The others in the room look delighted and all agree smiling nodding at the Minister who is now so confused that I realise that I am Sir Humphrey Appleton to the minister who is actually dimmer than his TV counterpart Jim Hacker. Reader Yes Minister was a brilliant situation comedy written and made in the eighties that is a relevant today as it was when first screened.

I, the corrupt civil servant manipulating a dim witted Minister. I really started to enjoy myself. I was starting to be visible and saw my reflection in one of the huge mirrors handing on the wall. I realised that time to make a strike and get out.

"What I humbly suggest Minister is that we increase the Arts budget and use other budgets in tandem to help our cause."

126

"What!?" explained my hit. He suddenly came down to earth with a bump. "Why would we do that when we have a duty from the PM to make massive cuts? I think we are going off point here."

"I agree. And that is your brilliance sir! You see recently when in charge of education you came under serious flack for the cuts you made. Mainly in the Arts departments in schools where schools were forbidden to buy or increase use of musical instruments and books on plays budgets cut. Now you can unleash this master plan of yours and show how you were merely lining up the greatest Arts investment in the history of the UK."

"I am? I mean I am!" he exclaimed and even Vesna looked confused.

"Yes sir, by taking the Arts budget and continuing you increase the reach to schools and the working men and women's benefits departments, then the cost can be evenly distributed through all."

Vesna looks at me and partly worried as this odious little man, who was a minister for the government was famous for saying yes then going back on his word and integrity was a word he could not spell.

"I am sorry?" he says. " What are you talking about?"

"I agree that there must be sacrifices made, but why does all the sacrifices have to be made by you? I mean to say, if you actually did this you'd be literally house bound, most hated man in the country." (He already is.) "Whoever gave you this poison chalice is trying to undermine your position should the top job come up."

My hit shuffles in his seat and awkwardly tries to convince the committee it was his idea to look into this and that the ex-mayor of London who was making noises now an MP again had suggested this to his rival.

I laughed and all looked at me as if mad. "I think I have a way to make the cuts and increase the budget and make sure the plaudits are placed at the right table, with the negativity easily fielded to other quarters."

The Minister looks to his watch and makes a gesture at Vesna.

"Well that sounds excellent. Good meeting everyone and I know the Minister has other pressing engagements so I shall email you all to reconvene and discuss new ideas and the proposals we can then take to further hearings."

The Minister stands and makes to exit and Vesna nods slightly nervously at him. I note that he is not happy, but intrigued to see what I will come up with.

As he exits the Minister walks up to me for a private chat. Informal, but revealing nevertheless.

"Sorry, all a bit confused there for a second as most of the others around the table, idiots who would not have a clue about the bigger picture of life like you and me. Have your proposal sent direct to me by tomorrow and look forward to further talks. And please do not worry about my position here, I have certain papers that secure my seat for life." He smiles at me, completely brazen. He literally could not wait to tell me he has a dossier on his colleagues that ensure he is allowed to do whatever he wants and no comebacks he will always be protected.

I now know that the rumours, albeit comical, are actually true. This vile little man has pictures of the Prime Minister having sex with a poodle, or something as bad, because there is no rhyme or reason why he would ever hold a post, let alone his seat. I suddenly see a bigger hit and bigger danger ahead. Sadly people disappear in the UK just as easily as in the Asian or Arabic World. Often knowing we are never safe reminds us of staying safe and exit routes.

Vesna comes up to me after he exits and looks as if to say, 'Who are you?'

"Well that was fun." I say and Vesna looks as if to say that she was in hell as she is terrified of the Minister. "You don't think it went well Vesna?"

We are alone in the room as everyone had left.

"Sorry, but I realise you are not Dudley Ramsden from the Arts Council. I was worried Dudley, whom I have only ever chatted to on the phone, may of been difficult to get on board, but he never struck me as... well like you have. I should have you arrested, but then they'll arrest me. Instead let me walk you out and you can buy me a drink."

I looked at Vesna who smiled and I did as she said. I was still inside the building and now very visible.

Walking out we see the Minister drive off in his official car. I see Vesna move into the shadows as it passes and I notice here is someone that is not happy with the things she sees. Vesna is my key to the padlock on the house, but she is a wonderful Croatian girl that I really do not want to get into trouble.

We make our way to the Groucho Club as I often go there under another alias I have and it is my favourite members club in London. It was a big celeb haunt that has been slightly taken over by city boys, but they are flash, ignorant pillocks that brag about things that to an Invisible are like gold dust.

Sat in the upstairs of the Groucho in a small area off from the bar I sit and chat with Vesna. She is off for the rest of the day. She smiles sweetly and then turns to me without a change in expression and asks, "So who are you really?"

I decide for the first time in years reader to tell Vesna the truth. I withhold my real name, but she is made aware of what I do. She at first thinks it is all in my colourful imagination to which I remind her of the fun we had earlier in the commons. Vesna smiles and nods appreciatively.

"God, that man is such a prick," and looks at me a condescending glance, "please, you know exactly who I mean."

I laugh and we relax. I told her the rumour I am investigating and if there was anything she knew to confirm or had she not heard.

Two gin and tonics later, "Heard? Heard? Seen the folder handed to security of the Work and Pensions

Nazi. I thought Croatia was now a right wing home of white extremists, but that bastard deserves to be given a medal to honour his indifference to suffering."

I asked what she meant and she stated that he was to be sacked and a new inner council of MP's all work for one main MP, the main Head of the New Order, seems a Free Mason based group, has a dossier collected on all his opponents gathered whilst not in the house. He holds all accountable to him and is making his move it seems, but each hold office without fear of loss as long as they do his bidding and that of the New Order.

I ask if she is referring to a former Secretary of State for Work and Pensions who carried out a brutal regime of cuts to benefits and essential support for the poorest in society as well as the disabled and sick or that idiot that was Education Secretary and every single teacher in the country hated with a furious passion for the damage he was doing to the education system?

Her reply with indifferent candour was quite simply, "Both."

My mission had become even more difficult and dangerous as with all secret societies they have the ability to kill, expel or make people disappear without ever worrying about possible investigation.

I would need to be completely invisible, yet I was exposed. Vesna knew me and I had been in the eye and on camera at the house for the hit. I know that men like them will always look into those around them they do not know, either to hold something against them or more importantly use against them for control. I had left the meeting definitely in control and that would not of gone down well. My hit was a nasty piece of work, but not stupid.

Vesna asks me if I would fancy coming back to hers for something to eat and possibly talk more. Now Reader please do not get ahead of yourself. Vesna had to leave Croatia as she was persecuted for being a lesbian. She wanted me to meet her partner and the love of her life, her dog. The barmaid flashes me a smile and I smile back to realise she is actually smiling at Vesna. Seems my Gaydar not working as well as it used to.

We leave the bar and Vesna tips the waitress who caresses her hand as she passes the change. I see the barmaid's outstretched hand and shake it saying 'Thanks' much to her confusion and Vesna's obvious pleasure.

"Come on you," Vesna calls as we exit.

As we leave I watch Vesna and wonder if this really is a blessing in disguise or is Vesna a double agent really to throw me to the wolves of the New Order. But I feel my new found friend is no Marta Hari, but a person that has endured far worse hypocrisy than the New Order and could possibly become an Invisible Woman.

20

Sat having tea and some wonderful cakes Vesna had made I am laughing and chatting with Vesna's girlfriend, Ana, who is a real joy too.

Vesna was cautious at first and then as I opened up and met Ana she realised I was not a spy sent to test her. It seems in the UK Parliament there is little trust of anyone for anyone. Where as boys we put books down the back of our trousers for when we got the cane, it seems politicians where chain mail vests to stop the knives in the back being a problem.

This mission was really a complete book of worms and the EU debate was where divisions were being made and the Head of the New Order seemed to be unknown, but he was a specter in the houses of power all the same.

Even the Prime Minister was in this dossier and for the time being he was not being lent on. Although, when he tried to sack a Minister from the New Order it seems it was not possible. Vesna herself was asked to drop off an envelope to the PM's office and seems by the time she returned to her office the spotlight was being placed elsewhere. Her man was being offered promotion.

One person who made a complete hash of the junior doctors and NHS was also unbelievably not sacked or even thrown out of the party. The PM feels that his party is invincible and cannot loose an election as he rules over the press, but within the battle lines are not at all clear. I must find the Head of the New Order.

Vesna had managed to keep hold of my ID visitor pass and so I was a dead end as far as a trail was concerned from today's meeting, but we decided to make me a new identity. I chose the Head of a group of dissatisfied BAFTA members looking to find a way to oust their corrupt and unelected committee. I was now Sir John Isaac. It seems I was never introduced as a name when in the offices and therefore not a problem to go in with new identity.

Vesna's mobile rings and as she stares at it she looks up frightened. It was our Minister the hit. She put it on speaker.

" Vesna. Who was that guy today from the Arts Council as seems he was not Dudley Ramsden?"

" No sir, Ramsden did not show and another guy, Isaac was there as a replacement."
" Find out who he is and I want to meet him tomorrow morning at the bar."

With this he hangs up and Vesna looks concerned. I smile and take the phone.

" No worries. Now let's have some more tea and more of these fabulous cakes."

Ana smiled and Vesna went to put on the kettle. I could se that she was worried and Ana looked as if to say to me, ' She is going to be safe isn't she?' I smiled and just looked towards the kitchen then to Ana, "Everything is going to be fine."

As I walked home I started to think about Ana and Vesna and their worried faces. I knew that if anything went wrong I would make sure I would be visible to make sure they are safe. Both had been through enough with the escaping their homeland. I would not want their secure life together in my favourite city jeopardised by me.

I had agreed with Vesna that she should say I was a temporary replacement and that I would be happy to meet the Minister. Armed with facts I now know I hatched a plan overnight and was on my way to Parliament and there at the gate waiting was Vesna with the Minister.

He had on a trench coat and a hat. It was like guy at a fancy dress party in the world's most stupid spy costume. But it worked, as it was so stupid he was invisible and we all walked into St James' Park a few hundred yards away. Sat on a bench by the main pond he looked me in the eye and asked my how ambitious I was. He was intrigued by my candour and approach and seemed when I said let others pay for our genius he was hooked. You see Reader, this hideous little man would like nothing more than to look noble whilst actually ripping someone else off. He would be happy making someone else the fall guy and rise in position thanks to their downfall.

Once I noted this he was mine. Greed is a really blinding force that enables me to show the monkey the shiny, shiny, with my left hand and fleece him with my right. I dazzled the idiot with my cunning plan to show how to make huge cuts by readdressing the funds from other departments. For example, all the new funding for film equipment and musical instruments would be found from Education budget, the new workforce required for the new improved Arts council from Work and Pensions and best of all the money needed to be raised to help fund new and rejuvenation of theatres in the UK from match finance from city brokers and most offered huge tax incentives. But lastly the coup de gras was the fact that the company that would financially benefit from the money spent could be a company that was owned by him in an off shore account. Now these last phrases, his company, offshore account, were the words that get these little misers really excited. I even suggested he put the money in Vesna's name so it does not trace back to him. He even took that on board and asked me if we could trust her!

I then asked that if there was a huge fallout within other departments against the proposal would he be in any jeopardy as I would hate that to happen.

" Don't worry my friend, I will always be fine, you see I have use of a certain document that gives me immunity." I start to wonder is he the Head of the New Order? Then it seems not and he says that there is one other he needs to discuss this with before final commitment. He laughs out loud to himself in a smug self satisfied way and openly says, " Well that little shit of a Chancellor is going to have a fit when this cluster bomb hits him." So Chancellor of the Exchequer not the Head of New Order either.

Mind you the current Chancellor must have his own dossier on the PM as his cock-ups and scandals recently helping his mates and bankers make millions out of incorrect sell offs of the countries assets made us all surprised he was not sent to the Tower of London, let alone not sacked.

Then I met the PM once and not much going on between his ears, so all that in breeding has led to a vacate mind easily coerced and that is just as worrying. He seemed aloof uninterested.

Reader, this journal is really a daily write up for you also to read and keep safe, but hope it inspires you to question the reality behind some of the strangeness we endure daily from our world. It may not be grammatically correct in its writing or prose, but I hope the style I write can be read and visual images are easily accessed from your own collages in your own minds eye. For I need you to realise that you can be an Invisible, do what I have done even on a smaller scale, just ask questions and ask why, without fear of being ignored. The more we ask, the more we learn, the more those that feel above the law and act as if we do not matter will soon be taken to account for their wrong doing.

In a world of so much corruption the arrogance we see everyday that affects so much in our lives would be less by just saying no. We have the power Reader to make a difference.

We can boycott shops where serial offenders own and avoid tax, and even bankrupt their firms bleeding the money out and feel they are not accountable. I saw in the news today one fat cat friend of our spoon faced liar PM avoid questions on how he destroyed one of the main high street firms he owned and walked away with millions in tax havens off shore, yet still has another company he abuses operating. Let's all not buy in his other top shop and for legal reasons do not name him or shop as it will not take much to see this crook for who he is. I say crook, he does it all under the umbrella of legal routes left open to him by his friends in power so he has no integrity, and even if the shops were to close we would hurt so many innocents sadly, but his bank balance would not be hurt. He is so wealthy may not initially hurt him, but his greed would not take it easily. Also we would ostracise his children who then feel they too can go on to behave in the same way, and thus stop future generations from workers abuse.

I though have a storm to brew and concentrate now on my greedy, power hungry MP and his gang to bring down from within. It will be difficult to orchestrate, but their lust for control and belief they are above the law will make it all happen I am sure one way or another.

21

I am on the search for the Head of the New Order and all I know is it is not the PM or the Chancellor or my hideous little allies I am meeting today. For today the two I meet are my Minister for Health and Secretary for State. Yes both odious little men are meeting me as it seems they are both in the New Order and have taken me in as their desire for fame and rub shoulders with the famous fuel them taking the eye off the boil and not look closer at me. Meeting a famous name has blinded them and they cannot actually see me; they just hear me.

Vesna sits in the corner of the park where we sit and have an outside coffee. I am amazed as no one notices us sat there, being joined by the other minister and realise we are surrounded by tourists as paparazzi and journalists wait outside Parliament for shots and chances to talk, whereas I have both at my beck and call. Mind boggling? Well read on.

It seems both have a pack to become PM and Chancellor at some point. Both have been putting out policies from the PM and then making a disgraceful hash of it. Although they look bad they are both ready to go through a serious redemption period in six months as the PM will be ousted by the New Order.

Both will say how they followed the party line and did what they were told, but now no more, they laugh as they can see the public rejoice and love them for being amazing and taking on the giant like two David's. They even have a pact that on the toss of a coin they will decide who becomes PM and who is Chancellor, but they must also defeat the man behind the New Order as he too has his agenda.

I jokingly remark that make sure there is no dossier on you guys and they both react. It is then they open up to me as their new confident, new ally and best friend.

"We need to get something on him as well. At present there seems to be nothing, but we will find it before we make our move to ensure we can even up the score."

The Minister for Health looks as his colleague says this out loud with a worried look on his face, but his friend continues, "Don't worry, I think somehow our friend here may just have a plan for us."

I look at them both and then at Vesna before leaning in to depart this next stage of my plan that has fallen into my lap.

"Gentlemen, I think you should make me part of your team and help me get access to the corridors of Parliament, with Vesna as my aide as well, and we will no doubt unearth something juicy before too long. In fact I will guarantee it, plus they will be watching us rejig the Arts and not know what our real mission is."

Both look at me like excited schoolboys. I am now in full Invisible flight as both listen, but do not look at me. I am grinning inside, as it is so easy.

"First the Arts. We set up a press meeting to announce more funds for Arts as wanted by the government's pledge. You'll quote tardy TV talent shows ripping off the Great British public and how you are going to make this nation the leader in the world of Arts. There is no money and the job was to cut the Arts budget and that is what you will do, but be taking money from other budgets, small amounts, but sizeable enough to enable huge benefits."

"Sorry, do not follow?" says the Health Minister.

"Hear him out, this is brilliant", squeals the Secretary for State, like a little boy who got all the cream.

"All we do is make donations to the Arts from all the other budgets that will help in their sectors. For instance, Education Budget gives two hundred and fifty million, about a few percent of budget for more Art in the schools, the Defense Budget gives five hundred million in order to make projects that help with their efforts to promote through the Arts to the people their needs."

"And we can make sure that the Member for Uxbridge area takes the blame as we can leak all this idea if it goes south as his." The two become so excited at the Secretary for States' betrayal that I now know who the Head of the New Order, the mastermind behind the blackmailing, thought of as buffoon, but hidden his agendas behind this facade.

" Gentlemen, let us get this paper written up and with a possible few billion raised make sure one of you or both are lined up to run the campaign and make sure the money is spent with those we want as quickly as possible and then I can spend more time in the house finding out something really career ending on the Grand Master, the Head of the New Order."

They have already passed me on the possibilities of what they can do with the money, yes you guessed it, blinded these two Uriah's with greed, that they do not watch or see me until suddenly Vesna joins us to makes a motion. I notice a journalist coming down the path and both look worried, but tell them to trust me and see exactly how well I can operate.

They both stand and the journalist is almost stopped dead in his tracks.

"Quentin," I say stepping forward. He is so focused on the two Ministers he does not even see me, "Haven't seen you since the party at Monica's."

The hack does not even know what I am saying as I put my arm round his shoulder and lead him to the side of the Ministers.

"We were just talking about you and thought that what we need is a serious person to announce something really big we have planned and you may just be the ticket, old chap."

"Sorry, do I know you?" he asked.

"Quentin, do I know you? I have for you the biggest leak since that little shit Wiki tit who had nothing, but a load of made up files that he got lucky on. We have a billion pound investment in the Arts about to launch, a whole new reshuffle planned and you could be the man we need to break it, but to get the whole story we need you to be prepared for a few weeks of secret meetings and say nothing."

"I'm in." That was it as I got the two ministers to nod and the eager little journalist was getting so excited with the thought of what he thought was about to happen he rushed off as if he was touching cloth. Sorry old saying I joke about with the twins to get them moving. The twins? My girls. You see Reader all Invisibles have a visible life as well.

As he dashed off two very worried ministers looked at me and I laughed. Not a chuckle, but a huge belly laugh. I looked at their confused faces.

"Gentlemen, I think you two ought to decide who is the next Prime Minister?"

They looked at each other.

"I will have contact via Vesna only so nothing comes back to me. Make me a fake ID and get it to be access all areas and within no time at all I will have information that will give you the cards to make you have the winning hand. Be like Blair and Brown all over again, except you two I think could share the role. Be a first don't you think?"

"Who are you?" asks one, "Why did we not hire you before? No wonder they love you at the BFI."

The two laugh and then regain composure before nodding each other and then walking off in different directions, but then unconsciously realising they are walking off in the wrong direction. There is an awkward moment and I whistle. Both look at me.

143

"Just cross the road and walk in together. Nothing wrong with two colleagues enjoying a harmless stroll together."

They smile and wave and soon are deep in conversation returning back into the commons. Vesna looks at me, and laughs.

"How do you do it?" she asks.

I shrug my shoulders and we link arms walking off back to Piccadilly smiling. It feels right with Vesna, and she tells me how she escaped Croatia and their right wing homophobic government and how she comes to England and sees the rise of another right wing regime forming. In fact she is concerned our two ministers are the wrong men to help as she fears they too are secretly so far right she would be living in a Croatian state again. Neither know nor realise she is gay and their views on homosexuality are quite extreme. Seems they both loved Elton John growing up and only after he adopted twins did they realise he was gay. Safe to say they don't play Captain Fantastic and the Brown Dirt Cowboy anymore. I love that album.

I assured Vesna that by the time we have finished she would not only see those two never make their way up the political ladder and her getting a position she can choose herself. Of course we can never truly predict all outcomes, but have focus and you can get there.

So Reader we have the two dreadful ministers whose greed and belief that they will be the next leaders, whilst thinking of how clever they are they will never notice half of what I will be doing. And yes I already know how to bring one down, guessed yet Reader?

It is literally two hours later and I get a call from Vesna and I am now meeting her in the bar at the Houses of Commons. I am now Sir John Isaac, head of BFI policy. I had given Vesna my picture and in twenty-four hours from our first meeting I was walking into the member's bar completely legitimately and able to move about freely, well as freely as most, plus I could use the offices of two ministerial departments to hide my activities. It was at the bar that I heard a voice I hadn't seen in ages and remember a case I had heard about being looked into by another Invisible Woman that this person had hidden. She disappeared and I knew the bad men of politics were still thriving.

I walked onto the terrace on the river to look down the River Thames sipping my American Champagne... Coca Cola, and heard him say that the power of City Hall would soon sweep through the Commons. I suddenly realised from this cocky statement from a man so evil he made Stalin look misunderstood, I realised that to compete this mission I would have to travel down river to City Hall. If there were skeletons then they would be hidden in closets buried under the cesspool the last incumbent had made it.

Vesna joined me and then I see one of the Ministers raise his glass to acknowledge me and I smiled back. Then in walked the Prime Minister himself, followed by the ex-mayor as usual cajoling and blustering his way through another pointless story, whilst trying to rub his elbow, as if by mistake, and rather bullishly, over the cleavage of a busty secretary minding her own business. It seems this is the subtle chat up line of an inbred moron whose belief that power is all you need to get into a woman's knickers. May of worked with a few of his

145

colleagues' wives, but this young lady was not impressed. She smiled as if no worries accidents happen and as his back turned made a face and gesture for all to see that she thought he was a complete wanker.

I smiled at her and asked the barman to offer her another drink as from an Englishman no lady should endure such sexist bullying.

I remember Vesna smiling at her too and then at me.

" I am happy with Ana, but to be honest had you not bought her a drink I would of."

I laughed and Vesna quipped, " So who do you think stands a better chance with her, you or me?"

" You, of course," I replied.

Vesna smiled and collected her handbag to leave.

" Liar," she said as she exited.

I laughed and saw Vesna pass the girl as the barman gave her girl the drink from me. Vesna passed and just before she exited turned back at me and winked.

22

It was 5am the next morning I woke. I thought I had blacked out as woke in strange hotel room not knowing where I was. I was in bed with the girl from the Member's Bar. I smiled as I watched her ample, naked bust heave as she slept. As I looked at her she woke and smiled at me. She was even more beautiful than I had remembered and kissed me. It was a wonderful moment as I obviously had blacked out before and not sure if we had done anything I would like to remember. Turned out we had and she wanted to relive the moment again. I will not forget that moment again. And here is one honest bit for you Reader, her name was Chastity.

I was drinking a coffee looking out the bedroom window and realised I was at the Tower Hotel. Apparently, one other perk of my new status was an all expenses paid suite so I could work close to the Commons. I had mentioned I lived in Waltham Cross, I was actually in my favourite neck of the woods Notting Hill, but did not want Ministers knowing. They were asking so they could set up this suite. After a few more hours with Chastity I was more than grateful that they did.

I was dressed looking out Tower Bridge as Chastity left and could see City Hall. My room phone rang. It was Chastity, she just wanted to make sure I had her number for the main parliamentary ball was in three weeks and thought we should go together. I of course agreed and added that I hoped to see her before then to which she replied, " Oh you will." That was some woman. I returned to look out over my next mission objective and whilst had my notepad in hand to write the phone went again. I wondered what Chastity wanted this time?

It was Vesna, she laughed and said that I should meet her at City Hall in twenty minutes and I agreed as it was less than that walking from where I was.

As I walked up to City Hall I could see Vesna in a tight fitting skirt and her long, wavy, brown hair flowing in the wind. It was as if we were in a perfume advert and she looked amazing. She turns and spots me then laughs.

" What's funny? Have I forgotten to do up my flies?" I quip.

" No, you look like a man who has had a really good breakfast." She replied and kissed me on the cheek.

" Well you look ….. hot? Is it Ok to say you look Hot?"

Vesna looked at me and laughed, " Why not? That was the intention. I have us passes and we are there on Ministerial business and need access to files on the Arts in London. If we are not alone then my appearance will distract the man or woman with us whilst you find something for us to use."

She was an incredibly confident woman.

" Oh and by the way, you'd better miss meeting the MP for Uxbridge as he had invited Chastity for himself. He was watching you closely, now he will be watching closer."

I realised I had become visible and would make sure next time I met the less than honourable gentleman he would

148

be with his wife. Always good to keep jealous men at bay by being seen as confident friend of their wives.

I put on my badge and laughed as we entered City Hall. Passed the public looking at the central stairway and we entered a door away from the public and were in a lift to what used to be called the Mayor's Lounge. It is a wonderful function room with great views. We were to meet Tobias, who was to take us to the records room and had some files for me to look at.

On cue in walks Tobias Ruffalo. Stunning six foot four young man in his early twenties. Vesna flashed a smile and he did not respond, but I knew I would fare better. I reached out and shook his hand holding on a little longer than I should of to see Tobias react with a slight double take and then flashed me a smile.

" This way," Tobias said and as we followed I joked, "Don't worry you bum doesn't look big in those trousers."

Holding the door open for us Tobias flashes a wider grin and says, " Best view is no trousers at all."

" Sorry, Hi," I said, " I am Sir John and this is Vesna."

" Sir John, well I hope you have a white stallion nearby." Tobias was now heavily flirting with me as Vesna whispered in my ear, " I hope he has a sister."

Tobias turned and grinned, " I have a twin sister."

" And is her hearing as good as yours?" I asked.

" I have no idea, but we should invite her over to make up a four, what do you think?"

I smiled and looked at Vesna, " In the words of Humphrey Bogart…. This is the start of a very beautiful relationship."

Before long we were all in the main record room and in the middle is a central desk and four computers back to back. It was like in a spy movie and Tobias decides to be outrageous and flirt so he bends over thinking I was looking at his derrière and had no idea I was memorising his log in code.

I removed my notebook and wrote it down and Tobias looked at me questioningly.

" Six four, thirteen stone plus, forty four inch chest, thirty-two inch waist and hips to be assessed," I quipped.

Camp as Christmas Tobias spins on his heels and sits smiling, he loved flirting and felt free to be himself.

" So, what are you wanting not already in the file?" he asked.

This computer room had every document and every secret that we needed.

" How about some dirt on the last incumbent of City Hall?" I jokingly said.

" Oh her," he said, "nasty piece of work. All classified and apparently team coming in to overhaul the computers next week, but I think he is having them cleaned, there soon will be nothing of his double deals anywhere."

" Homophobe. Met him last night and let's say not been a fan before I met him or after. So who is coming in to clean?" I said.

" Some junior minister looking to make his way up the ladder." He said.

"Actually that'll be Quetty, tall French and very beautiful. He has promised her a special position if she pleases him. To date she has not accepted any positions with the creep, but she has been given the task of coming here next week," replied Vesna.

I look at Vesna, as does Tobias, and she smiles, " Well, while you boys are watching each others asses I am watching hers, and I watch all the lower female aides looking for promotion. Quetty is great and incredibly stubborn. She was furious in the ladies as he touched her breast reaching for a book and he apologised with some crass remark. She would love to get out of his office, but to get out, even slip out under the door she'll have to slide under him first."

" Shame it's all being destroyed then," says Tobias.

"Yes, shame, as be great to have something as a keep sake." I replied.

There was an awkward smile and I looked at the file Tobias had given us. In it was a list of all the main theatre companies and directors and noticed ticks by some.

"What are the ticks?"

"Oh they are friends of people we know and they get invites to parties and we send details of grants to apply for…"

"But what about those with no ticks?" asks Vesna.

"Honey, no tick, no click. They would never give a grant to anyone who'd produce work that may question them or be politically bent against them."

Vesna looked and pointed out to me London office for the theatre company in Scotland in our first papers. Why would this small theatre company in Scotland, Inverness Players, have offices and company address in London?

" I think we will have to read this Tobias and come back to you tomorrow if that is OK?"

" I agree Vesna, but first let's all have a lunchtime gin and tonic."

Tobias's eyes light up and he flashes a huge smile.

"I have just the spot. Out of the spotlight so to speak as to be honest if they see me in gay bars then my career would stall and this would be it." As he walks off for us to follow I feel a deep sense of pain as here I am conning this really nice guy, who everyday has to hide who he is in order to be accepted. This is the 21st century!

As we exit City Hall Tobias takes us to a small member's club called The Men's Room, which also accepts women,

152

just the name was there before the club. It is full of men in suits and women chatting at the bar.

"We all come here, all know each others secrets and the women are not all gay, but they do like to be somewhere where the men do not think they are play things. It is a truly patronising world for a woman to suffer, so tell me Vesna, what makes you love to suffer?"

I look at Vesna and she sighs.

"I have no idea some days, and other days like today, well that makes it worth it."

Tobias looks at Vesna and me and then gets up and walks to the entrance, " One second."

Vesna asks me for my notebook. I hand it to her and in it she writes six numbers.

"The door code to computer room. I have been repeating it in my head constantly since being in City Hall. Was going mad thinking and about to forget. Gin going to my head."

I look at Vesna and realise what a truly special person she was and for the first time on an invisible mission felt I had an ally. Tobias returned with two passes for the club.

" Sir John, Vesna, it is V E S N A is it not?"

Vesna nods and smiles.

"Good, everyone here only has first names and often they are not real, but thought to give you club names may be a bit too forward on our first date." Tobias looks directly at me.

"Sir Jim is perfect," I reply.

" What?" exclaims Tobias. I show him the pass has Sir Jim and not Sir John. " That bitch at reception has always been jealous of me! He did that so you'd think I couldn't remember your name, stir it up for me."

"Well, I like Sir Jim, so let's have no more said OK? This is a wonderful G&T and let's enjoy the moment."

"And here's to many more moments to come." says Vesna who seems drunk on just one G&T.

"Blimey!" says Tobias, "that was a double but we'll have to watch our little girl from now on."

We all laugh and again I am in gratitude to Tobias who unwittingly drew my attention to noting best not let Vesna have too much to drink.

I helped get Vesna home after leaving the members bar at one, that is one in the afternoon. Ana was in as she was working on a thesis and looked at me and sighed, "Gin and Tonic?" I smiled back and we put the wonderful Vesna to bed.

This gave me a chance to chat to Ana. She was writing something up on the reasons to stay in the EU. It was for the Huffington Post and have to say her account of the horrendous plight she and Vesna suffered made me realise how great this country is as we do show the world we care. Of course other countries do as well, but I left Ana to walk back to my newly paid for suite and walk among a country full of colour and beauty. Even loved the fact a skinhead male was in a doorway passionately kissing his black boyfriend. Now that was different, but not really, this is England.

News of another horrific gay killing in Florida hit the headlines and again politicians call for the death of all Islamic Muslim Terrorists. All except Obama the out going President and saw a post on social media that read one cartoon character asking another,

' Why didn't God stop the shooting? '

To which the other replies,

' Because God doesn't exist. Engage with reality and fix your fucking gun laws.'

23

There is a real sense of uncertainty in the air as I walk back to Tower Bridge. It is a decent walk, but through some of the greatest architecture in the world. I love London. I avoid Parliament and walk down the Strand to see my old friend John Barr who is in a new musical based on the songs of Anthony Newley. John is one of the greatest characters and best voices I have ever heard. He knows me as Andy. I wasn't sure, but luckily he saw me first and called my name.

We had a coffee in the Waldorf Hotel and it was nice to catch up. When John was trying to rebuild his repertoire up he used to run a late night cabaret in Leicester Square. It was fun and I managed to convince him to make a CD and then I managed via contacts in San Francisco to get it sold there as it was sold only in a shop, sadly no longer with us, called Dress Circle.

I am so pleased for John's success as no matter what is going on in life one constant ray of sunshine is John Barr and his support for others. Only 5'7" and I am being kind, this small in stature, big in heart, musical theatre actor and amazing voice, is possibly pound for pound one of the greatest performers we have in the West End today.

It is nice to meet and be me, or be Andy, or Sir John or one of my many guises, and just sit and chat. Listen to others and interact. As an Invisible Man often we are never seen, as I write this upon reflection I realise that I am more than visible. Time to start to work out next steps.

I call Chastity and I take her to see John in his show and then dinner after at Joe Allens. It is a great night. I know I was broke a few days ago, but now I have expense account and hotel paid for, go figure. Mainly as even though I may be living as another person I am always honest with those I am with. I am sat thinking of plan to get into the file room again as Chastity complains she has been detailed to help some Foreign Bird next week clean an office.

Could this be Quetty? No it turns out to be a Polish Girl in my new hits office. Polish it turns out called Malgorzata Harper. You can't make this up. She is referred to as the Megstar. Family call her Meg, or MK or Malgosia or Gosia, this girl has more names than me. Sorry how do I know this? She shares a flat with Chastity and we went back to hers as she could not wake up at mine again due to she thinks she is being watched.

Yes Reader, she might sound paranoid, but the married MP from Uxbridge is stalking her using the police at taxpayers expense. This is a minor cost compared to the millions he spent or wasted on egotistical schemes that never happened, but he got to travel the world researching. It seems I also have to be more careful. Questions were asked as to who I was and can Chastity find out more about me. I enjoyed the next bit.

You see I then decided to tell Chastity to explain that I am the Cultural Arts Expert that reports directly to her Majesty, the Queen. I would love to see the look on his face when that information hits him. As Chastity and I get into bed I see on the floor a webcam. Chastity sees it too and says that she found it in her room and Megstar saw it in the bookshelves so they faked it falling over and faces into the carpet. It seems my Member for Parliament likes to exercise his power to webcam illegally and exercise his member whilst his wife sleeps.

" Still, keeps him faithful," I joked as we all sat on the bed chatting.

Chastity was incredible, but the raw animalistic draw of the Megstar was phenomenal too. She not only was tall, slender and had the most amazing legs reaching up to the perfect bottom, she was highly intelligent. I could see why she had trouble making her way up the ladder at Parliament.

It was 5am and I was sneaking out of Chastity's bedroom to see Megstar sat at a table drinking tea. She had a very sheer sexy negligee on and little else.

"Sorry did I disturb you?" she asked.

"Not at all as need to get back to hotel for a shower and get ready to formulate plan for the Arts."

"Fancy a cuppa before you go?"

"Yes sure, builder's bum for me."

"Breakfast tea it is then, sorry but, I don't have a builder's bum," she joked and I had to say to myself, 'No you most certainly do not'.

We sat drinking tea chatting and suddenly it was 7am. Chastity broke our conversation as she was up. She lifted my arm, looked at my watch and headed off to the toilet.

Also learned that Megstar was going to be on leave so Quetty would be going to City Hall alone. "

It was really nice meeting Megstar who got the name from other junior ministers and civil servants, as she was always one step ahead of the others. Every minister and head of one organisation or other had tried to bed her, but she would rebut them and instead of finding herself doomed to a crap job to do, got promotion. She would literally do it in such a way as to make them decide it would be a foolish mistake and that in best interests she should be put in charge of over seeing some big project.

Chastity returned from the toilet and gave me a kiss. She then looked at a picture I had noticed of her and a handsome young man. Megstar looked away as I pointed it out and Chastity looked forlorn.

"It is my fiancée. I am sorry, but we are having a break as he cannot deal with I have a better job than him at the moment. He works at 10 Downing Street, but is one of the lowest of the team there and just makes and fetches tea and biscuits. I am a minister's aide and as such get better pay and more privileges. I am sorry Sir John, but I am a little lost."

I was a little taken aback, but this is the modern day and they are on a break, and look how well that turned out for Ross and Rachel, Friends, well even in real life the two are not best buddies with David not being invited to Jennifer's wedding. I have taken pride that I have never cheated on anyone and never cheated with a girl on her boyfriend... well knowingly. I stand and give Chastity a big hug.

"Had I known I would of not of ….. well I am not that kind of person. Listen, please do not feel ashamed, just tell me about your man."

Chastity is taken aback and starts to cry. Megstar just looked at me the same way Marjorie did on the flight and it reminded me that there is always a reason to do the right thing. Chastity opens up as Megstar hands her a hot cup of tea and kisses her gently on the top of her head before sitting next to her holding her hand.

"His name is Henry, Henry Ballantine. We were on the intern program together. He was a graduate from Oxford and I was a graduate from Exeter. He thought he was the one they would choose as he aced every single assignment given, and I scraped through. I enjoyed the process and then one night he took me out after a long text correspondence where we talked about how we both just wanted to meet someone, have great sex and no embarrassed conversations. We sort of sexted and one night I said to come over and he did. I opened the door and he just kissed me and within twenty minutes we were in the bed, well on the floor as we missed the bed, but couldn't stop. We both were called in and told we had got through the assignment. I was ecstatic, but as we were told separately I thought he had not got it. He thought the same and so we gingerly left the building and went for a coffee. Slowly he looked up and said that this was such a sad day for him. I started to cry and he hugged me. I remember saying something like I wished they'd chosen him instead of me and he sat bolt upright and looked in amazement. They did choose me, that is why I am sad, but you were chosen too. It looks us a few minutes to realise what had happened and then both let out huge screams and acted like two overgrown, over excited school kids. It was one of the happiest moments of my life. And now I had ruined the ...." she starts to cry then looks up apologetically, "Sorry I love the sex with you too, but I realise I am in love, shit I am confused."

Megstar looks at me and I hold Chastity's hand.

"It is all fine. It will all be all right. The only three people that know of this tryst are you, me, and the old Megstar here." Chastity smiles.

"This is what I propose. We have a memory of a wild moment and move on. I am old enough and ugly enough to survive and you need to see this young man of yours and ensure he knows that you do not want to be on a break. Never tell him and if he ever finds out or hears anything tell him you acted as a foil for me as I am gay. "Both girls laugh. "Trust me, it'll work."

"But I want you now." I look at Chastity as she says this and make a facial gesture and follow up with, "Is this because you feel guilty? Seriously just do not loose what you want and I do have one condition though."

Both look at me.

"You are working on the clean up at City Hall with Quetty are you not? So I will sort out for you not just Henry, but make sure you'll never be on a break again. Oh and another thing, sorry condition. You must tell Henry that you want to move up ladder as well, but no competition as if you can be happy for him he will be happy for you."

"Deal," squealed Chastity.

"And you have to let me take you out for a truly amazing Polish evening to show my gratitude."

"Oh Megstar you are the best." And both girls hug.

I notice Megastars beautiful long slender and perfectly toned thigh and said out loud, "You know what I think you are …. both of you, the best, best of friends and best of … well best of the best."

I wasn't feeling awkward, but felt sounding awkward the best way forward. Forward for what Reader? Well for the situation of course.

"Listen, I need a shower," says Megstar and I almost said I'll join you, but stood, hugged her and then Chastity and left.

Walking back to mine I passed Heaven, the gay club under the arches and there I saw, well I thought I saw in a wig, the Chancellor of the Exchequer. Trust me Reader it was him. You see one thing you learn as an invisible is how to spot those trying to be invisible. The glasses and the dodgy wig were no match for my trained eye. Really funny as without even realising I was making a video of his coming out of the club with what was possibly a rent boy. There was suddenly security and they were not for the club or police. They looked like secret Israeli Police. The rent boy was in fact the son of the Israeli President. Oh well, another time as to be honest it may do me some good, but if people want to live their lives how they want then I want to let them. Here they are not harming anyone, but I hope somehow the Israeli makes our Chancellor put on a gimp suit and beats the crap out of him.

It was 8am?

24

I get a call and it is from Chastity to say Quetty will be visiting the City Hall next Monday. I smile and think it is about time I meet this Quetty. I reminded Chastity to call Henry and make sure he is primed for them both to go to the Parliamentary Ball. I can hear her smile in her voice as she forgets what she was going to tell me and I remind her, so it is set I am to meet Chastity for introduction to Quetty prior to City Hall on Monday.

It is now Friday and the days have gone fast. I decide to try my new pass out and go to the bar at the Commons.

Ridiculous as this seems Reader, but I am there at the bar drinking with this fabulous under secretary, Chelsea, and in walks this vision. Tall, ebony faultless skin, beautiful eyes and I start thinking is it me or are most of the secretaries hired by the Tory ministers stunning, except for the wives? This vision walks right up next to me and asks for a screwdriver. Now here is the best part, she asks for it in the sexiest French accent on earth.

"Quetty, if only I was a driver.."
Quetty looks me up and down and suddenly Chastity arrives.

"Quetty, this is ..."

"Sir John, here helping with the new Arts Budget."

I offer my hand and Quetty takes it and smiles.

"I never sleep with the men I meet here."

I look at her as she fixes me a glare and as quick as a flash I reply to her, "Neither do I." Chastity laughs out loud as the Barman brings over the vodka orange, "Screwdriver?"

"Not for me thanks, but thanks for the offer."

Quetty looks at me as the penny drops and she laughs, "You wanna 'screw' driver? Chastity, I like this one."

"Seems everyone does," Chastity says under her breath.

"Listen ladies I think we'll see each other again no doubt. Off to City Hall." And with that I exit. I feel Quetty watching me and before she knows it I am gone and walking through the corridors Invisible.

Standing at the top of a set of stairs I suddenly realise I have no idea where I am to get out of there and a group of men come walking towards me all trying to get the man in the centres attention. He stops and looks at me.

" Hi, you lost?"

I look back and reply, "No Prime Minister, well maybe a short cut out would be appreciated."

The PM looks at me and laughs, "This is why I have all this security with me as to be honest I have no idea where I am."

We both laugh and I see this is not a bad person, just power has consumed him. We walk together down the stairs and the two Ministers come out of separate rooms at the same time and see me with the PM. Both stop and try to hide in the shadows as we pass. The PM is focused on moving fast to the next room he is in, so he does not get ambushed by someone with a searching, but uninteresting question.

"That way Sir John," the PM points and I see the exit. I smile and thank him and within no time he is whisked away. I am impressed at his observation skills and I am sure he saw the two ministers lurking. This place makes Game of Thrones look like a children's story. I was glad to get into the street and enjoy the cloak of invisibility once more.

Walking to City Hall again I was starting to strut as thought I needed to perfect a walk to stop Tobias watching what I was actually doing. I am walking into the main doors as Tobias is exiting.

"Meet me in the club in ten have I got news for you." Tobias is overjoyed at some news.

"Actually, I'll join you now."

In no time we are in a small corner of the bar in a booth that is dark and foreboding. Sort of booth you know gangsters would use or people discussing hiring hit men. Complete with curtains and screens.

"Well, apparently, last night in Heaven…"

"The Chancellor of the Exchequer was seen with the Israeli Prime Minister's son," I finished his sentence.

"Oh you heard the rumour already?"

Now I truly dislike the Chancellor. A truly disagreeable man whose fortune and privileged has him his position not his brains. Had this been the PM I had met earlier I may of thought twice, but no I enjoyed this.

"No rumour my friend," as I whip out my mobile and show him the video.

"Who's the guy in the wig, he looks dreadful?"

I look at Tobias as if to say look again.

"Oh my giddy aunt, that's... that's..."

"The Chancellor of the Exchequer?"

"How did you get that?"

"Listen if ever you have troubles or are victimised at any time let me know and I'll send you a copy." Tobias gives out a mighty laugh and all look at our booth.

"Honestly you two, if you cannot get a room pull the curtains," says a portly old queen.

We both laugh and Tobias says he has a boyfriend in Libya he is worried for as not heard from him in ages. Tobias starts to cry and I realise the danger his boyfriend must be in. I wonder why he needed to tell me?

We sit in silence for a few minutes and then I say that I had better get on with the files and off I walk leaving a truly lovely guy worrying about his lover miles from home.

In City Hall I manage to get into the main rooms and the code to open computer room of Tobias's works a treat. I sit at the desk and start to look for files, but soon find that it was not going to be that easy. It seems many of the files were security encrypted and to be honest thousands of files and I have absolutely no idea, which one was the one I was looking for. I scan the room and try to see how I will get files before destroyed. I think a trip to Park Lane required and make sure all turned off as I exit.

I was walking down the SouthBank and racking my brains how to remain invisible without alert suspicion and hoped that there was something worth having. I still wanted to get lucky and find the dossier compiled by the Head of the New Order.

I ended up walking all the way. It was a beautiful day and the walk is a good way to focus thoughts. Much of my thoughts kept drifting to Megstar and her long silky thighs. Come on Reader don't judge me I am only flesh and blood. I want to write everything here for you and feel that this journal only works if I am completely honest.

The duty of all Invisible Men and Women is that they must remain honest and true in every situation. What that means is that if you have something that can harm a person's reputation then you must only use if it serves the people. Invisible People do not act with malice.

Walking down Piccadilly past Green Park and then into the bottom of Shepherds Market, the true prostitute haven for those of wealth in London, hookers fetching £2,500 an hour, I find myself soon passing the Playboy Club and see the infamous Lenny Beige exiting the club. He is lining up to perform there again and I cannot praise highly enough reader seeing this great artist live. He is performing and has guests Fingersnap of the incredible Guy Davies and David Mcalmont on stage. I think this is where to bring Megstar. Beige greets me with a hug and a smile.

"Hello my old friend, what the feck in all that is Jewish are you doing in town?"

"Lenny, I am on an assignment and seems will be down for the show." I say.

"I can put you and guest names on the door. Call me you old tart," and with that he is gone.

Lenny, real name Steve Furst, is possibly one of the best comic actors ever to grace a stage. A legend and if you know Lenny you have a friend for life.

Things are looking up as I enter the spy shop. A small establishment with gadgets galore.

" Dimitri, I thought it was you," comes from the manager walking towards me, " What you looking for? You know I got it?"

I have been coming here for years and the manager; whose name escapes me remembers everyone. I know that once I exit he'll forget me as he suffers a weird form of memory loss, but once he sees your face he remembers names.

"Hi, listen cut to the chase, working for British Secret Service and need to extract files from a computer without plugging in. Can get in the room and even log on, but…"

"Say no more Dimitri have the thing," he says. "I have a little device, hard drive, you just place it next to person downloading and the device downloads without them knowing. This one looks like a cigarette lighter, a Zippo."

"But sadly that may not work as I want to download before they are deleting."

"Same thing is as they delete files this copies and also copies encryption so that you can open on any computer anywhere. Brilliant no?"

"Amazing." I ask how much and he says that they are £1,500 each. I tell him I want three and he offers me a discount.

"My friend, " I say,"The British Government will pay so no discount required.

He laughs, "In that case I charge you double and give you extra in cash, sort of cash back and why not use Russian Diplomats card so they pay as idiot try to steal from me?"

We both laugh and I exit with my three Zippo lighters and four thousand five hundred in cash.

As I walk down the street I see Jimmy, ex-Royal Marine living on the streets. He sees me, and Jimmy who used to be Invisible too until he made an error and was seen after exposing a crime boss in Dubai. He lives on streets and hides, as price on his head is seven figures, Royal Saudi family embarrassed. Even MI5 been trying to find him.

"How's it going Jimmy?"

"Tough mate, but got a fun consignment in tomorrow so a few grand coming in."

"What have you got on you now? I ask.

"Sorry friend, broke."

"Liar," I said and hand him a grand. "Stay low Jimmy, stay safe."

I leave Jimmy speechless and walk off. I see him look up but I have disappeared. I smile and before I can look back he has gone too.

Jimmy was one of the best. We both hit the same mission without each other knowing and as we exposed a sex slave group we were able to confuse the police chasing us as they thought we were part of the gang. Both of us in a room no way out full of coppers and yet both walked out unnoticed. He was one of the best, I just followed in awe. He had Jedi like mind skills, for there was no way of explaining how he did it getting us out.

He exposed an Eastern Block Nazi Group drug running and sex traffickers. The mob were actually grateful to him and managed to have one fraction of the mob unwittingly help him escape another group as he played informant on the other to start them infighting and get girls out safely.

25

I can now relax and have a good weekend. I am at the Tower Hotel and in the lobby spot two security men linked to my ministers and realise I was not alone there. Without being seen I walk up behind one and eavesdrop his conversation saying that once they see me they'll escort me to the bar.

So you guessed it Reader, there I am behind the bar with the two ministers sat watching the door I walked in through on bar stools looking at their watches.

"Gentlemen, please tell me you are looking for me?"

Both almost fall off their seats and look as if to say what you doing behind the bar. I hop over the bar as the two security guards come rushing in.

"Gentlemen, I have good news." They walk me to a table behind the piano on a plinth. We sit and both look at me eagerly.

"OK, let us have it."

I smile and tell them how they must arrange a meeting with Quentin from the paper on a week Thursday. I remembered this was the night before the Parliamentary Ball. I had a plan and it was now going into place with this being stage one. I was not expecting to do this so soon, but they turned up and had to give them something.

"I will have a dossier for you gentlemen very soon to protect you and bring about changes at the top if you

172

know what I mean? Each department in the government will give a small amount to the pot. It will be the biggest funding body ever in the Arts history. No one will note that they have donated and once they do will all believe they will benefit from fund double back what they put in. Of course you both will be the instigators of the fund and move to jointly oversea the spend, and we are talking billions gentlemen with travel to meet with stars and even co-produce with Spielberg even. I see you both having to spend a lot of next year in Hollywood, Sydney, New York, Paris..... Well you will have the lifestyle of billionaires and be seen promoting British talent. Simon Cowell is nothing more than a cheap version of Chuck Barris. He was the original creator of crass TV for the masses with his Gong Show, and Dating Shows that had huge viewing figures and little intellectual presence, but it made him millions. You gentlemen will be helping present Opera at Versailles to two hundred and fifty million dollar movies that will mean you would be the most powerful men on the planet."

"Oh I don't know about that.." squirmed one as if embarrassed.

"You can be PM I'll be happy to see out my days in Malibu," said the other.

Sometimes it really is like taking candy from a baby. Then the baby just keeps giving.

"You know I have my own theatre company in Scotland that is a tax haven as used to hide funds. HMRC think it is a dormant company and is a conduit for me to cipher off funds. I can show you how to set up and even use the PM's father's contacts," starting to laugh at the brilliance of his scheme he adds, " he still has no idea it was me that shopped him to papers. That secured me as Deputy Head of New Order."

"Well if you want to, I mean there is going to be so much money no one will know where any of it went apart from what we disclose."

"Waiter, waiter, bottle of Chivas please. Lets celebrate."

"They do an 18 here. Make it the 18 waiter and some nuts."

With that the two were toasting themselves and their geniuses without even questioning any of the mechanics, just greed took over and that Reader is the way to truly manage a hit. You can shoot them from the front and they still do not see you pointing the gun.

I left them saying had to do some paperwork and disappeared into my suite. I also took the opportunity to ask for the suite to be changed so if they came for me they'd go to the wrong room. Another plus side to my move was the other suite had a jacuzzi. I do like a Jacuzzi, don't you Reader?

26

Saturday at the V&A Museum, cannot think of a better place to while away a few hours. Been a member on and off for years and such a un-costly place to join. You get free admission to all exhibitions as well as go as many times as you like, not queue and relax in tranquility. I am here and just wandering about aimlessly as so much has happened in such a short time again and I need time to recharge my batteries. I see walking towards me in the main fashion hall Megstar. She looks amazing. Coincidence? Oh come on Reader, I said recharge the batteries and the company of a beautiful, intelligent, engaging, did I say intelligent? Well a stunning Polish woman always has my attention.

She kisses me on the cheek and smiles.

"Are you OK?"

I look as if to say yes, but then realise she thinks I am upset over Chastity.

"I am fine, more than fine, in fact happy as you are here. To be honest once I knew she had a man it was over for me. I truly cannot cheat on or be a part of a person that is cheating, I know she and Henry were on a break, but…. And to be honest when I saw you I was a gonna anyway."

I held Megstar's hand and we walked off to the coffee area and think she liked me, but was little overawed at what I just said.

"Let's take things slowly and expect nothing more than what we have now." As I said this Megstar hugged me and kissed me on the cheek then full on the lips. She stopped looked at the coffee shop and just said, " Patisserie Valerie?" It is in Knightsbridge and with two grand to spend, although I was still using my government credit card as it seemed to have no limit, a short walk from the museum and we were there. The walk was even a joy. Passed the Brompton Oratory and decided to pop in and look at the ceiling and friezes. Her knowledge on art, politics, cars, pet handling, fashion, music... she could talk on any subject and was as confident as she was beautiful.

I suddenly realised I had no idea what she did. I decided not to ask. Had the most wonderful cakes and tea and strolled past Harrods and towards Hyde Park then decided to do something spontaneous. Megstar looked at me as if I was mad, as she never does anything spontaneous I felt and in seconds we were in a taxi off to the SouthBank and managed to get the last two seats on the Duck Tours. A tourist trip around London on an old amphibious landing craft. It was one of the most fun things I have done in a while, but also without realising when finished we were a short walk from Tower Bridge and my hotel.

On the SouthBank I noticed a man watching me. He was obvious and felt he wanted me to see him as shortly after he walked off in the other direction. Megstar was oblivious, she was high on life. I think the day was just what she needed.

Back at my hotel we sat in the bar overlooking the bridge and she asked me how come Chastity and I got together? She wanted to know what I liked about her?

I explained that one minute we were at the bar in the House of Commons and the next minute I woke up in bed in a hotel suite I was given, also unknown to me at the time. I had no regrets as she is a gorgeous girl, but feelings were lust and once her revelations of Henry I realised it had just been a wonderful moment, but the feelings had gone.

I said that I would be more inclined to take the next relationship a lot slower. I confided that I liked Megstar, realised she was a trophy that all the ministers chase, but never catch and yet happy to not know her story.

This could be a fatal mistake in the line of duty as an Invisible Man. But I was truly for the first time falling in love. What the hell is going on?

We both held hands and looked each other in the eye and agreed to take things slowly. It was as if I blacked out Reader as the next moment all I remember is being in bed making passionate love to the woman of my dreams. Not only was she incredible in bed she loved to talk dirty in Polish. It sounded rude, but sadly do not know a word of Polish except thank you, pronounced Gin Queer; well sort of.

I have always learnt how to say thank you in many languages and thank waitresses and waiters in their language at every chance.

Now Reader, this time I did not blackout and remember every detail, but I am an Englishman and as before I never discuss such matters. Just to say that in all my life I have never experienced such deep all encompassing love. Lust was there, but fuelled my love. I tried to recite Shakespeare at one point and she laughed as I got it wrong and thought I had deliberately made the mistakes.

I looked at her and asked what she wanted to do tomorrow and she laughed and pointed to the clock by the bed. It was only 4:30 in the afternoon. Well a movie then?

I go to the bathroom and hear Megstar's mobile ring and she answers.

"Sure, of course I'll come. No not doing anything at all. Give me an hour and we'll go to the cinema."

I exit the bathroom and smile. "Got to go?"

"Yes," she said as she should up from the bed naked and she took my breath away. "It was Chastity and feel things did not go well with Henry. Can we....?"

"Of course we can," I replied and handed her a towel robe from the bathroom door I was stood next to.

Reader I have to say I am smitten, which is a real problem for anyone looking to lead the Invisible Life. Megstar was effervescent and perfection in every way. OK great body, great smile, intelligent, way smarter than me, speaks five languages, funny, great company, considerate of others, wait a second she is coming out of bathroom.

"Oh my God! You take my breath away." Megstar just stops and smiles putting on an earring.

"What you writing?" she asks.

"Just a Journal of an Invisible Man." I say, yes reader I was typing this as it happened.

"Make sure I sound good won't you?" she quipped, "do your best."

I got a kiss on the cheek and then she was gone. Fate would have it Chastity then rang me. I answer the mobile and there is a pause.

"Chastity, is that you?"

"This is Henry, who is this?" came the voice on the other end of the phone.

"Henry? Oh Henry, the love of Chastity's life. I wondered when she would introduce us. I heard so much about you."

"You have?"

"The internship and both getting through, you in the PM's office, well done you, and she with the idiot I am working with. You did know we are work colleagues. Oh my God Henry you fool! The girl is in love with you. Did you think..? Oh come on son, I am old enough to be her father. Well don't tell anyone that."

" I am so sorry, this is so embarrassing."

"No it is not! You should be proud of yourself and that you were ready to fight for her, you old romantic you Henry. Listen, tell that girl you love her, break the on a break off and tell her to meet you at the Hilton in Park Lane and then go to the reception and tell them you have a booking in the name of Potter, Harry Potter. Trust me it will all make sense if you have the balls to woo her back."

"How can I trust you? I don't know you."

"OK Dopey, two questions. Do you love and want her? Do you really give a flying, well does it matter who I am? Go to the Hilton, go to reception and let fate take its course. OK?"

"OK. But if this is a ….."

"Wind Up? You'll know when you get there and take a chance on love Henry, be spontaneous. Remember tell her you love her and all will be fine."

"OK. I'll do it. Thanks." The phone went dead and I smiled and then took out my government expenses card.

Dialing the number to the Hilton my thoughts went back to Megstar and she was just about to…. "Hello Hilton. Oh hello. Have you got any suites available tonight and tomorrow? Plus meal in the room tonight and breakfast to be determined by guests. The room must be in the name of Mr. Harry Potter. Have two bottles of Dom Perignon in the room chilling and a table for two in the main restaurant for seven o'clock tomorrow as well, but an option of having dinner in the suite as an option for Mr. Potter and his guest to determine. Have you written this all down, then type it up as a schedule for Mr. Potter to have on arrival and please deduct from my credit card for everything. Yes I have the number here one second.."

Yes Reader, I have just booked the most spontaneous and romantic weekend of luxury for Chastity and her man. I recommend that this is a course of action all couples should do now and again. Obviously you do not have to hit the Hilton Park Lane, but a cosy little BnB in Appledore, North Devon or a chain hotel in Harrogate, just say be ready woman to have weekend away and do it. Or even Prague, Budapest, Paris the list is endless. If it was me I'd…. I am thinking of Megstar again, this is hopeless. I must get my mind on the plan, a plan that I still have not sorted.

The door knocks to my room. It is Megstar.

"She called me to say she had to meet Henry at the Hilton and he was insistent she went with an overnight bag."

I smiled and Megstar looked at me then out of the window, then to me again, and said, "It's no use I have to tell you, I am starving take me to dinner." What a woman.

27

I sit at the desk in my hotel suite looking over the Thames and at the array of ID's I have. For the Ministers I was Dudley Ramsden from the Arts Council posing as Tyrone Butterworth to work covertly for them, and also at City Hall I am Sir John Isaac. Now to all I am Sir John. I smile, as at times on this mission I seem to have trouble remembering who I am. I had managed to sleep with an amazing junior assistant for my hit, but then found out she had a fiancée and yet managed to part without difficulty, and even managed to get her and her man, they were on a 'break', back together, but my greatest moment came from finding myself in a relationship with Megstar, the junior assistant's flat mate.

Now Reader as an operative for the Invisibles relationships are sort of a no-no, but this Polish beauty with brains to match was just, well, I am smitten. Love does come when you least expect it and it seems things are going to become truly complicated.

I am alone and I receive a call from Vesna that the ministers want to meet. Seems the Head of the Order wants the Arts policy out asap as he intends to damage the Prime Minister's popularity and he is furious not done as instructed. Seems they want to publish the initial dossier and yet their greed has kept me in the game.

I agree to meet at Parliament. This at first frightens them as they want to meet somewhere clandestine away from the eye, but I explain that the best way to be invisible is by doing everything right under their noses. You see if we go about as if just going to work on new

Arts policy no one questions why, we meet in secret and wherever we go people will see.

Vesna calls back to confirm and also that the Minister wants me to conform to his idea of meeting in Parliament and the Common's Bar. I look to my ID passes and grab both Tyrone Butterworth and Dudley Ramsden and bin. I wear Sir John as that is the one that will get me in the Commons passed security, as it is legit now. I walk in and visit the gentlemen and walk into the bar. I see Quetty there and we smile at each other.

Quetty is very much like Grace Jones. Tall, dark, sexy and flamboyantly dressed. In walks my two ministers and Vesna and I am motioned to join them at the table. We are no more than a couple of minutes into the meeting when the MP for Uxbridge enters and a few MP's smile and offer to buy him drinks and he sees me. Quetty walks over to him and they make their way to our table. Both Ministers stand and shake his hand.

Nervously the Education Minister starts to introduce me, " Let me introduce.."

" Sir John," I chip in and confuse both, except Quetty who says, " Sir John, nice to meet you again."

I had my ID badge in view and all look at me.

"You know each other?" asks the Head of the New Order as I now refer to him.

"Quetty, always a pleasure." I reply.

"Yes we had a drink here, he was funny." Quetty said in a flirtatious way and yet condescending manner.

In walks Chastity and seems perplexed then sees me and her bosses and then the Head of the New Order. She walks over with a fixed smile.

"Sorry late sir I was not expecting your call on a Sunday." Chastity looked glowing and I stood up and shook her hand.

"Young lady, thank you so much for looking after me the other night. I think I was very much worse for wear and sharing the taxi was just too generous."

The Head and others look at me, and Chastity smiled. I continued, "I thought you had big family thing this weekend? Surprised to see you too."

"I was called ....." Chastity was interrupted.

"My dear girl, you should of said, listen our meeting can wait until tomorrow, please my apologies will have my car take you back to your family do."

Now even more confused all looked at the Head of the New Order as he seemed to be trying to be chivalrous as if in competition with me, and this made the others nervous.

"Hilton was it not?" I asked.

A confused Chastity said, "Yes," then looked at me.

"Well don't keep them waiting, the car," I smiled at the Head and shook his hand.

"Well nice to meet such a gentleman, and are you joining us for a drink?" I follow up.

I knew he would not sit with us as he knew he had given the two ministers the most damaging public opinion dossier for the Prime Minister to deal with and would not want to be associated.

"Another time," he replied and then shook everyone's hand and left poor Quetty standing alone.

"Quetty, would you like to join us?"

Quetty smiled at me and looked at her Boss leaving. He was by the door patting his pockets. Quetty bends down to pick up some keys on the floor.

"Sadly no, I think someone has lost their keys again."

And with that Quetty went off to hand the keys to her grateful boss who then answered his mobile and went out the door. A young junior minister was sat on his own and Quetty went up to him and whispered in his ear. He smiled and they exited together. I was looking forward to meeting her again. Intrigued to find out what she said to the young junior minister.

My thoughts were broken by an unhappy Minister, "What was all that about?"

"Oh not to worry, he will not remember he met me and no idea who Sir John is and by the time he knows what has hit him he will be so confused he will not even remember you two. And anyway gentlemen, you'll be his boss." I raise my glass. "To the new Arts budget."

It was funny as they raised their glasses and toasted along with me. That night we hatched a plan to meet with Quentin on the Thursday night with the story; the news with break Friday and we would all be having a wonderful night at the Parliamentary Ball.

28

Sometimes reader it is so opportune to get a mission that you can actually go on knowing not only if successful you'll make a difference, but also for a cause you truly believe in. For me this was one of those such missions. I was as happy as a man about to go to bed with the most beautiful Polish woman. Of course I am grinning like the cat that got all the cream, but I still have to carry out the rest of my mission and it all depended on precision timing.

You see I feel that the Arts are completely under appreciated, as the Arts are the lifeblood of any countries happiness. If this or any government had spent money on investing more into the Arts the rewards would of been tenfold. The reason they do not is because by supporting the Arts they are giving money away that does not go towards their own pockets.

You see I once was behind supporting a primary school in Willesden where the Headmaster was the most extraordinary man. He wanted to put a radio station for the children in his school. An outlay of six thousand pounds and also wanted a music room and instruments from his budget. Well after fighting for it he boldly placed both into the school. The result being his pupils aged 5 - 11 were more polite, responsible, great vocabulary and conservationists, more out going, confident and when children went to middle school from his primary everyone knew they were from his school. It was life changing to see the little children develop into little people with amazing people skills, hugely multicultural and all developed into understanding and appreciation for their fellow pupils no matter what religion or background. This is what the Arts can do.

We watch tawdry talent shows on TV making millions off the public and then using and abusing those they say they will help, yet if we funded and developed at schools and universities to the same investment, we the country would benefit greatly, not just in producing better, well rounded and happier people, but financially as they would in turn earn in some cases bankers wages.

But it is not just for the gifted that the Arts is so important. This government wanted to kill all Arts funding in schools and decided to form more Academy schools funded privately and owned for profit by their friends, but they failed miserably in their first year. They decided that all children must stay at school until they are 18 instead of 16 and not be allowed to leave until they pass rudimentary maths. Now not every child is good at maths, not every child likes maths and although I enjoyed maths having it forced upon me made it less attractive.

Many children are dyslexic or gifted in other ways. Often if you look at business world leaders none of them were academics. By giving all children access to music, poetry, the theatre and film helps them develop skills that are far more important than knowing 17 time 17 equals 289.

They learn how to talk and interact confidently. They learn how to be better than others in areas and be as equal as a person with A levels in Statistics. They write and produce music that unites people, they make films that move us and make us think. The Arts are the greatest tool to keep check on those in power as they can relate to the people and what they are thinking and bring people together to discuss issues as well as just purely entertain and make us all feel good.

Sorry Reader if starting to waffle, but just take time to think that if we deprived you of the chance to make music, be in a band, express yourself either through dancing or interacting with the music? Where would you be without great films and theatre? Think of the money the Arts generates without war, war being the biggest money earner for most governments. With Arts we can keep peacefully an eye on the powers that run the country without violence and inspire a nation to come together to help those that need help. The Arts have always been the greatest weapon man has produced to unite and fight without killing a people to understand there is more to life than what we are given.

This is why this government wants to Arts subdued, because the Arts will mock them and through satirical TV to films by greats like Ken Loach and Mike Leigh, Shakespeare's of their generation, that held the governments of this country accountable. If there were no Arts development where would the next generations happiness come from?

This is why fate has place me on this mission and whatever the outcome if the Arts are beneficiaries then that would be a success to me. Although I have a cunning plan in order to achieve this and silence the New Order.

I am again in the hotel looking out my window at a car parked outside with special branch officers sat in it. I see Megstar arrive and they are not looking for her, yet, but I start to feel guilty as if this goes bad she may become involved. I am once again reminded why Invisible Men and Women lead lone lives. I had fallen hopelessly in love and on a mission that I could disappear from, but the one I love could not. What am I to do Reader? What would you do?

There is a knock on the door and I answer. My love walks in and kisses me then sits on the sofa.

"So tell me when did you meet Henry to sort out the weekend?"

I smiled and forgot how smart Megstar truly is.

"I got a call from Chastity telling me everything and then I got to thinking what made Henry change so drastically in under twelve hours of you knowing.....?" She stopped and stood up. In one swift move she undid her dress and let it fall to the floor. She looked amazing.

"I think I am not going to be able to know what to do with you soon," she said.

"Champagne in bed?" I quipped.

"Later may be," she replied.

There is a knock on my door. I wake and realised I had blacked out. I was on the sofa naked and Megstar had left.

I grabbed a towel robe and answered. It was a special branch officer. He looked like an assassin.

"Duncan Ramsden?" he asked.

"No, sorry Sir John Isaac, can I help you?"

"Sorry Sir John, have you ID?"

"Sure, come in, what's all this about?" I hand him my ID for Parliament and he looks at me and then apologises and exits.

I knew that something was seriously wrong and that the Head of the New Order only knew me as Ramsden only. My smart-ass behaviour had managed to make me visible. I knew I had to make an exit and forget this mission, but I would also have placed Megstar, Chastity and also my new best friends Vesna and Ana in the firing line. As I stand there looking down at my flaccid, naked self, I wished I had been more loner and not become involved so easily.

I look to see it is 8am and get into the shower and dressed. I also check out and using my government card withdraw five thousand pounds in cash. I book into the Dorchester. A small suite at £1,800 per night and pay cash. I call Vesna and tell her what has happened, but do not tell the Ministers as they may get spooked, but can she make out the other credit card I have was stolen and have new one issued and meet me at a cafe by Embankment Station.

Sat having a coffee I see Vesna walk out of the tube and towards me then walked into the coffee shop and watch as she bought herself a coffee. I did not move as she gave me a look to say 'do not move.' I feared she was being followed, as did she.

I finished my coffee and looked around as Vesna finished hers and motioned me to look at her table. She left her purse and exited. I saw two men follow her from across the street. I was now extremely scared for her.

I collected her purse with the new card on top for me. I chased after her and pushed past the two men following, almost knocking one to the floor.

"Miss, Miss," I called after her, " You forgot your purse."

"Oh thank you," she replied and made eye contact with the two men who then started to walk away in the other direction.

Under the breath she whispered. Meet me at mine in fifteen minutes, Ana is waiting. With this she hurried off and I was then able to stop the two men following to apologise and in doing so gave her time to become invisible. The men looked annoyed and said no problem in Eastern European voices, as they dashed after her and realised they had lost her. They looked back and I was Invisible. They could not see me watching as they sped off to jump in a taxi.

I rushed to Vesna and Ana's flat to find a worried Ana waiting. I hug her and comfort her that everything will be OK as Vesna walks in. Ana runs to her and hugs her.

Now I think that I have bought this upon them, but know things are always related somehow, and this was not a connection I expected.

Now Reader, do you remember Jimmy on the run from the mob? Well the mob he helped were cracking a sex trafficking mob and drug runners in Eastern Europe. They were a nasty group and wise that Jimmy is cautious, but also Jimmy had another mob group that wanted them dead and Jimmy had set up a sting where they all got caught by Interpol. Well, and stay with me Reader, Jimmy had two girls just caught up in the net and they were Vesna and Ana, who he helped escape. This is why Vesna knew so much about Invisibles and never said anything as she thought I may not really be an Invisible, but looking for Jimmy and them.

Once they relayed their story and I mine we had another mission to fix. I was scared for the girls and also did not see how Jimmy would of left them in the frame. I tell the girls to sit tight and I would chat to an old friend. Yes Reader, I need to find Jimmy.

Back at the Playboy Club I see a doorman that looks familiar and then realise it was not Jimmy. A voice behind me whispers, "He don't half look like me don't he?"

It was Jimmy. We go to a small bar opposite and sit down.

"Listen Jimmy, not got long, but you left two girls at risk in Croatia and your Mob friends are on the streets of London. I just bumped into two tracking the girls."

"What the lesbians?"

Jimmy was never subtle. "They have found one, but need your help to contact your mob friends to help out."

"I can't," said Jimmy, "The whole group were wiped out three months ago in a huge explosion. I think our eastern block buddies were at the route of it, but until now no proof. Listen I think I can help, but need to get into Special Branch."

"Well they are following me so let's do this now."

I am walking into the Tower Hotel and see the men looking for me sat by the reception. I walk over to them and tap one from behind,

"This way gentlemen, we need to talk."

Both look nervous and confused and then follow. We walk into the bar and sat at the piano is Jimmy. Jimmy stands as one reaches inside his jacket for his gun.

Cool as a cucumber, I mean Jimmy is the best, looking like an unemployed docker, Jimmy stands and walks over,

"No need for guns boys, thanks Nathan (That was my name he made up on the spot) I will take it from here. Gentlemen we realise that now is the time we at Interpol and you guys need to work together. Part of a Croatian Mob has landed on London and are starting to set up business. They are on our missing list and Nathan here has been undercover watching for them as they look to strike prominent member of the government. Now here is their names and faces from a few years ago. Go back to your headquarters, hand over file, take all the credit I do not give a shit, we will disappear and keep an eye on them whilst you get the team to find them and eliminate the threat, OK?"

They look at the file and as if they had been given a James Bond-like assignment nod and say they'll be in touch.

Jimmy smiles and laughs. "Just like the old days fella. In fact better keep on the move as I want Interpol to find them before they find me."

We hug and Jimmy exits. That was the last I saw of him.

29

I return to Vesna to find she had to go to work and Ana was distraught. I gave her a hug and conveyed what I had done. You are an Invisible then, for real?" she said. I smiled and said yes, but Jimmy and I would be keeping them safe.

I called Vesna to have her call Special Branch to find out who had been following me, do it under a different name, as they would not tell her, and tell them to tell the operatives that their suspects would be around Parliament Square at 6pm. I said that she would have to trust me. Ana shouts in the background to Vesna, "Trust him my darling I love you."

I find out that the two girls were the ones to help trap the mob and sadly through police stupidity they were asked to identify the mob in a line up where they could be seen, and that the two women courageously pointed out all of the gang. They knew it placed them in great danger, but they did it to save the girls trapped in houses all over Europe. I later read in a dossier that over six hundred houses, some in Ealing, others in capitals all over Europe were raided and over eight hundred girls released from a hell I cannot even imagine.

I hugged Ana and asked her to come with me and took her to my suite at the Dorchester. This is where I left her and headed to Parliament.

On route I called Quentin to meet me and the ministers on Parliament Square about quarter to five, and bring a camera crew. Quentin is a real media whore and loves to see himself on TV. I was not surprised he said he could be there earlier if I wanted.

I arrive at Parliament and as Sir John I enter. I am met by a really pale looking Vesna and I walk her into the minister's office. My makeshift plan is just about to go into action.

It was 5.30pm and Quentin bless him was waiting with camera crew and I saw the Special Branch boys all over the Square. It was hilarious to me as an Invisible I saw Jimmy and a few other Invisibles I had met via Jimmy and yet they could not be seen by anyone. Yes Reader, one was posing as Big Issue seller and two others as homeless, and on camera I could not believe it, Jimmy. How, I have no idea and to be honest never even knew he could operate the camera. I thought I would not see him again.

Jimmy looks to see and holds his ear. One of the homeless has spotted the mob lookout. I have Quentin set to go live and the ministers are prepped, but they have no idea what really is going on other than they will be seen as heroes. Vesna looks at me and then recognises Jimmy. I hold her hand and she realises to say nothing.

We see the mob lookout on his mobile and Quentin starts to chat about what it is he is going to be discussing. Laughable as it may seem, Quentin is so excited about being on TV with an exclusive live link he forgets to ask what it is about.

" Anti-terrorism in action," says the Health Minister.

" Sorry?" says Quentin.

197

Jimmy sees the mob arrive and they are missed by the Special Branch, "One second, be on in five." Jimmy says and motions me to assist him. "Get Special Branch to cover Churchill Monument they are all there and shooter is by church."

I look to see all about to happen and fear for Vesna then call to the Ministers to call Special Branch. I motion to Big Issue Invisible who has already moved to take out shooter. Special Branch man arrives and I explain where everyone is from mob and he embarrassingly acts on the walkie-talkie and I look to Jimmy he should turnover the camera and action.

Confused Quentin looks to camera then the Ministers, "Sorry what's happening?" One minister pulls Quentin to the floor and the other wrestles Vesna down. Jimmy and I film the whole thing. The shooter looks to aim and Big Issue Invisible hits him with his magazine copies to the back of the head and the gun goes off. Jimmy films the Special Branch rush and capture the mob after a short burst of gunfire before being shot. No casualties and no one except the mob hurt.

I help the ministers up and they look to camera as Jimmy then moves to film when I am out of shot.

"Quentin, thank you for joining us as we were to announce the new Arts budget, but that will have to wait until tomorrow as my esteemed colleague and I heard of a plot to shot the Prime Minister as well as kill our amazing assistant here and we placed our lives at risk to prevent that happening."

"And we are glad to say that all went well," says the other minister, although really shook up they did well. I was proud of them. Meanwhile Jimmy turns the camera to Quentin who is on the floor crying curled up in the fetal position calling for his Mummy!

I motion to both ministers to help him up and they do so. Police and Special Branch come running over and start applauding. The camera keeps filming; Jimmy has gone as have Vesna and I. We see all the gang dead or badly wounded and in the melee we escape.

I have Vesna at the Dorchester with Ana and answer her phone. It is the Prime Minister who wants to make sure she is OK. I explain that the Ministers had her and partner placed in safe location and were at the Dorchester. I told the girls to sit tight. I knew the Prime Minister would be on his way trying to bathe in the blaze of glory.

I handed Vesna a note saying that the Interpol operative that had bought them there had gone, but that he had been assisted by a junior assistant that would be introduced to him at the Parliamentary Ball.

I left and just in time as in the lobby I passed the Prime Minister who noticed me but was whisked passed by security.

Reader, you must visit the Dorchester lobby as the smell of flowers is overwhelming and watching three security men from the PM sneezing all in tandem was so funny; it was as if they were under attack from a pollen terrorist.

I manage to slip out unnoticed. In the note for the Prime Minister is a small explanation about Ana and Vesna and that they should be given new identities and protective custody to be rehoused and set up in Venice as part of a protection plan. Ana and Vesna met on a holiday in Venice. They received £150,000 a year and a fully secure hotel they owned in Venice to run as their own business as cover. The new names they took were Camilla and Tulisa. Ana thought Camilla was a tribute to Jimmy as his mother's name, and Vesna had always loved the name Tulisa. In the first week of opening the famous Italian actress and beauty, Antonella Salvucci stayed and gave a wonderful revue. The hotel became a huge success and even had Jimmy staying there as concierge. I will visit one day, but first we must get back on track with the mission. But that was after something that I had to sort out later in this story.

30

My two ministers were beside themselves and now huge heroes and I had inadvertently made monsters into greater monsters. They thought they were unbeatable and I could see that this had affected the stability of the New Order. Even the PM was in the bar toasting them with members of the opposition joining in.

Another funny thing is although there are different parties with completely different views, at the end of the day they all get on with each other and the game is to see who can they get to pay for the drinks. Don't worry, they don't pay; it comes from their expenses that we pay for through taxes.

This was Monday night and I saw Henry in the bar with Chastity and I smiled although remained distant. I saw my two boys; my ministers recounting their heroics and no mention of Jimmy and I so all good.

Quetty was looking annoyed being bombarded by offers to buy her drinks and with her a young black boy looking out of place. I noted that Quetty had a call and looked annoyed and said to the lad, eighteen, to wait for her as she left the bar. I was curious so went to chat to the lad. His name was Michael and was her friend's son. Quetty had sort of adopted him after her friend hit drugs after a really abusive relationship. Michael was a bright lad and was looking into which college he should attend, but he needed to fund the university fees himself as he was from Ghana. I told him that often things come up that no one can explain and things will work themselves out. Quetty returns and is surprised to see us chatting. She is quite off at first as she does not like anyone getting close to her and then mellows as she sees Michael is happy with me. At first she is upset I know something personal about her, but realises that I am not after her for anything, but conversation and a chance to become acquainted. She needs to get a promotion to afford Michael's fees and so far, she tells me after three drinks, most opportunities for promotion come from having to lay on her back and think of England. Quetty tells me of her scheme to help more students reach university and afford scholarship programs that mean more access for the poor and tax relieve for companies that sponsor. She is trying to get it heard and then also help Michael.

She has stayed at the same level for some time and luck would have it the PM sees me again and maneuvers to the bar to say hello.

"Hello, excuse me butting in, I seem to keep seeing you in the most sensitive places. I'm the Prime Minister and I have no idea who you are?"

"Well this is Quetty and she has the most brilliant scheme to help not only more youth afford college without loans, but booster your popularity at the same time." The PM is smitten with Quetty's beauty and then calls to his wife to join us. The entire bar watch and again I am not invisible. The Prime Minister's wife is actually really charming and I introduce Michael and Quetty. Michael tells his story, such to Quetty's dismay, but I then spot the opening as only the Invisible do.

"Prime Minister, if I may be so bold as I am not looking for anything here myself, but could there be a chance for Quetty to bend your ear for half an hour to explain quickly in detail her idea?"

"You can have our full attention now," said the PM's wife.

Quetty stutters and then looks at me.

"Basically it is giving big banks and corporate firms a wonderful tax write off if they sponsor students to college. The money we do not hand out to have students in debt will be praised and the tax cuts on the wealthy will be seen as acceptable, and let's face it there are more than a few people I am sure can come to mind that would like to support this new initiative you can roll out in no time at all."

Quetty looks at me, "There are certain criteria, but basically Sir John has put it in a nutshell." Quetty laughs and it is as if a great weight has been taken off her shoulders.

"I think it is a wonderful idea," says the PM's wife.

"Obviously I will need a closer look at it before...."

I interrupt the PM and say, " Of course, but first you should have her on your staff. Do it as an in house promotion so no one can object."

"That depends on Quetty? I mean do you want to come work for me Quetty?"

"Yes Prime Minister, I would be honored."

"Good that is settled then and for the first time in ages I can truly say I have enjoyed a drink in the Common's Bar," laughs the PM's wife. "I think we are going to be good friends too Quetty as I can already see the merit in your idea."

The Prime Minister shakes my hand and then Quetty, who hugs him and then goes back to shaking hands. The PM's wife gives me a kiss on my cheek and smiles then hugs Quetty. All the bar watch as Michael stands, "It was a pleasure meeting you sir."

"Michael, it was a pleasure meeting you and feel you are about to become the first incumbent of a new overseas bursary. Quetty, my office, no, come to number 10 around nine tomorrow morning and the kids will be out and I am sure my wife can make you tea until I get a moment."

"Yes Prime Minister." And with that the PM and his wife exit and the entire bar turn to look at Quetty who squeals with delight. Then composes herself and gives me a hug. I see Chastity watching and she looks a little jealous. I smile as if there is nothing going on and then realise I am now in a relationship with her flat mate.

I do not know about you Reader, but this has all become incredibly confusing.

Quetty then asks me what is she to do as she is meant to be at City Hall for her boss at 11:30am and he is not an easy person to get on with. Behind his public profile of loveable buffoon it seems he is a vitriolic bully and a truly nasty piece of work.

I see Henry at the bar next to us, and Chastity watching still. I call her over and turn to Henry.

"Hello Henry, I hope you enjoyed Harry Potter this weekend?"

Henry looks to me and I smile.

"Say nothing, it was my pleasure and it seems you and my lovely new friend are back on track."

"Yes, but how did you know about me?"

"Henry, I made a pass and she rebutted me saying she is in love with another and then over a drink she tells me about you. I thought I did not want you two to end up old sad losers in love like me at my age. I was right. You love each other and never be afraid to admit it. Oh by the way this is Quetty, she'll be working with you with the PM soon."

"Hi, I'm Quetty and this is Robert."

"Well I'll be making you tea. Sorry, just I seem to be stuck in career stall and....." says Henry.

"I know exactly how you feel," said Quetty.

"Let me buy us all drinks," I say, " and lets have them on the terrace."

Henry calls Chastity to join us and Quetty is for the first time relaxed and Michael and I are in full swing talking about football. Chastity is uncomfortable at first and then Henry tells us all how proud he is that his girlfriend is not only beautiful, but the breadwinner for the pair. Quetty laughs and bonds with Chastity who smiles relaxed. I give Chastity a hug and whisper in her ear, "You look radiant and back on course for a great life with the man of your dreams and as far as me I will always have the Tower Hotel."

"And Megstar," she whispers back.

I smile and she kisses my neck without anyone seeing, "I will always love you, but Henry is my true love."

I feel great and Quetty, a little drunk, guard down as ecstatic with her night smiles at me. I see the young man she left with the other night and I excuse myself to have him join us. Quetty gives him a huge hug and tells him her news. He seems happy, but non-plus. The girls go to the toilet and Michael gives him a hug.

"Robert, I may get my scholarship and thanks to him."

Michael points to me and Henry looks at me as if to say 'who are you?' and I start to get Robert to talk. Invisible Men are listeners as we learn from what we are told and often trying to impress people with stories about your self often are not the way to be popular. Not that I am looking to be popular just nothing can be done if you do not know what is needed.

Now in conversation with Robert it seems he is in love with Quetty, but she has a better job than him and so on.

"No worries my friend, join the club." Henry laughs and the two bond as the girls return.

Chastity looks at me, "What have you boys been up to?"

"Well I realise these two have phenomenal women in their lives, who both earn more so they could become men of leisure, but both still having the difficulty of realising how lucky they are. Robert, Quetty is amazing and Michael loves you too, so I reckon you are to be the envy of the whole House of Commons and Henry knows how lucky he is. Listen I have a little fun to help us all."

"You are too much, sir. But before I go any further the idea of the scholarships came from my talks with Robert when we were at mine discussing Michael." Quetty suddenly feels guilty claiming the credit for the idea.

"It was your idea that I added to..." says Robert.

"Good, I'm glad we got that settled," I say as if to say 'Just listen'. "One second," I spot something in the bar and rush in leaving the others wondering where I was rushing to. The PM was in another discussion with one of his ministers as he obviously forgot that is why he was in the bar and his wife looked bored. I tap her arm and ask her to join us. I return with the PM's wife and all look a little shocked.

"Well you all know this young lady," referring to the PM's wife, "Ma'am.." the PM's wife laughs as she is now a little drunk, "Quetty you know, Chastity who works with the bore the Secretary for State, her boyfriend, no sorry fiancée, Henry who works at Number 10 for your old man," the PM's wife laughs again, "Michael you know as future leading light, and genius as already found out he is a West Ham fan, and more importantly, this is Robert, who collectively came up with the idea Quetty outlined so succinctly.."

"Well, you did," said Quetty.

"He was succinct I'll give you that," says the PM's wife.

"Well it is also jointly Robert to thank." I say and the PM's wife smiles at Robert.

"Can you note that both Robert and Quetty will be coming tomorrow morning? To your husband, by the way he was the Prime Minister wasn't he?"

The PM's wife gives out an almighty roar of a laugh and the Prime Minister sees us all on the balcony. I watch him nod and make his excuses and comes to join us.

"Oh darling, it'll be two tomorrow," says the PM's wife as he looks confused, "This is Robert who also is partly responsible for the graduates funding idea."

The Prime Minister shakes his hand enthusiastically, "Wonderful, quite brilliant idea and look forward to breakfast on me as we discuss. Did you tell anyone else about the idea?"

"Education Minister and they thought a non starter," says Robert.

"I am surrounded by idiots," the PM says under his breath, "but I feel we have more than a few future cabinet stars here I'll wager."

"And this is ..." I start to say.

"You work in number 10 don't you? Henry is it not?"

"Yes, Prime Minister," Henry replies.

"Well see you all tomorrow and thanks you for keeping the wife amused, she is the love of my life and feel guilty bringing her to work. Got to get he home as we like to see the kids in bed and asleep. Night."

And with that they leave and are gone. I turn to look at my friends and all are speechless and stunned looks on their faces.

"Well that went well, didn't it?" says Robert and all laugh and hug each other as I slip off and enjoy invisibility once more.

I am walking out of the bar and halfway down the corridor when I hear a voice calling to me to wait up. I turn it is Henry.

"I just want to say thank you." He hugs me and I hug him back like a father hugs a son.

"Actually opportune you and I are alone. I have a secret mission for you. Friday morning meet me here and will hand you something I want you to give to the Prime Minister. You must hand to him and no one else and then take all the credit saying that this was found by people you had working for you. Chastity said you always wanted to move into diplomatic security operations, I hear it is better paid that Junior Ministers."

Henry looks as if he is unsure.

I will tell you everything on Friday morning and either you take it or not it is up to you, so all we are doing is meeting. We shake hands and I exit.

31

It is Tuesday morning 7am and I am up and showered. Ready for today as for all my mission to work today is the day. I am nervous as always. I think if I was not then I would not have the adrenaline pumping and the relaxed, possibly cocky nature would lead to me making a mistake. I already have special branch, Croatian Mafia, and other people all watching me, well three aliases I have concocted, but also my main fear is on Friday and I need to disappear what do I do about Megstar. I have fallen hopelessly in love.

My phone rings and it is Vesna.

"We are off tonight and I guess we owe it all to you. Who were you? We have been offered new identities and have been set for life. The idea the government came up with for us with the witness protection plan was like we had written it ourselves then Ana said she had a chat with you before all this and... hello, Are you there? Sorry just so happy, scared a little, but we owe so much to you."

"You owe me nothing except to make sure you enjoy your lives. You have told me enough I think to find you and one day I will. I owe you as if you had not done what you did when you realised who I wasn't I would be inside.."

"And we would be dead," Vesna cut in.

"Hello Father Christmas," I hear Ana shouting.

"Ana sends love too and that is our name for you and we do not need to know your name just you need to know you

211

are loved, got to go guys at our door to take us to train, Ana hates flying."

"Go and be safe and see you in a few weeks." She hangs up as I cannot finish what I was saying, but it is immaterial Reader. You see each day could be our last and we must live our lives, not watch others living theirs. I now know exactly where they will be and I will see them again.

My mobile rings again and it is Chastity, " Quetty is going to City Hall for 11:30 and told her you were working there today. You are, are you not?"

"Yes, should be popping in to carry out rest of my report on the Arts. How is everything?"

"Well Henry is now a little confused as no one in politics helps another like you do.."

"I'm not in politics."

"True, but he wonders how we met and then I realised from the way Megstar was singing in the shower I told him. You are seeing Megstar."

I knew Chastity knew, but was a little concerned how she would take the news.

"Well life often throws curve balls," I reply.

"I am sorry about us." Chastity seems sad as if she hurt me.

"It is fine as for me you are with the one you should be with, your true love and happy for you. I am old enough and ugly enough to understand life often is complicated and we have to adapt to the perimeters we are set. How was the weekend?"

"So it was you! Well sorry to say it may of been expensive, but it was exactly what we needed and planning a house and how we would work out work situation if I was the better earner, he thought that if Denis Thatcher can do it...... mind you I do not want to be compared to that heartless... I digress. I am happy for you and Megstar and as long as we all can keep the whole truth confined to abridged version I feel..."

"Chastity, unless you shout something out in anger then everything is safe. Now thanks for the update and I hope to see Quetty at City Hall. She is in with the PM so hopefully if there is a change of personality I will cope. Be safe and chat soon."

" See you at the Parliamentary Ball," she shouts and with that hangs up.

The Ball, yes the Ball Reader that was something I feel I would miss. Often as an invisible you miss seeing the moments you helped create and that is the hardest thing. You often see things change from the public viewpoint, but often-internal struggles dealt with and no one truly sees, but those are the fun ones to watch.

I have my black suit and dark navy shirt on and then decide that as I am meeting Tobias possibly a pink handkerchief in the top pocket. I actually think I look good. That is something all should look to do each morning Reader, accept ourselves for exactly how we are, unique, individual and special to someone. May be not everyone, but like yourself as there are always things to like about yourself. I always look for the good in others, easy to find bad traits, but look for the good in you. We cannot change who we are, we can change how we look sometimes, and I do not mean surgically, but we can treat ourselves and that is just as good. As an Invisible you must be happy in the skin you reside in. For if you are trying to be someone else you will be seen, a phony is always visible.

I am off out the house door and walking to the tube. I am now staying in an Air BnB in Chelsea. It is a nice flat and my host is a wonderful guy called Jeremy, an artist, and he hands me a sausage sandwich with tomato sauce. He knew I was off early so he made me packed breakfast as we got on so well last night.

Walking down the embankment the sun is shining and I look for a cab, but the traffic is slow so decide to catch the tube.

It is as I am packed in like a sardine on the circle line I realise a slow journey on a cab would of been a better choice. I smile at an elderly lady and then see a young girl with a badge saying baby on board. Both standing and see five seats occupied by city boys. They just sit there and ignore the women.

I am sorry Reader as if you want to see an Invisible visible then often this is the occasion. I push past a few people and find myself standing in the aisle. I am still invisible, well to the five city boys, but not the gentleman whose foot I trod on pushing past. I look at him and smile, I then decide as the train stops in the tunnel as moment to speak.

" Ladies and Gentlemen, Firstly, my apologies to the gentleman whose foot I stood on to stand here, but today is 'Be a Gentleman Day'," all look at me as if to say what?

" Now I am looking for two, no three gentlemen to stand and offer their seats to this young lady, the elderly lady always falling over with her bags, and this young lady who is pregnant."

The whole carriage smile and all look at the five city boys who look up as if to say what? Two immediately stand and I start to applaud and the ladies graciously, if not a little embarrassed, say thanks to them and sit.

"What are your names guys?" I ask and they reply Peter and Christopher.

"You see we had the greatest known saint, Saint Peter and the patron saint for travellers, St Christopher with us today. I did say I needed three seats," and another city boy stands, "What is your name my friend?" I ask.

"Terry." He replies.

"Well today will also be known as St Terry's Day," all applaud and I turn to a little Indian lady, "Ma'am this is Terry your knight for today and he wishes you to have this seat."

She is a little shell-shocked and takes the seat and a little tear hits her eye. As she passes Terry she gives

215

him a hug and all cheer. Everyone applauds and shout with me, "For England and for St Terry."

The other two also look at me, "And of course not forgetting St Christopher and St Paul." The train lunges forward and all fall into each other and start laughing and cheering. I see that Embankment is the next stop and decide to exit and walk the rest of the way. As I get off and walk past the carriage I see women getting on and men standing offering them a seat. Simples, is it not Reader, simple. I walk above ground feeling happy with the days start.

It takes me, as I walk fast, about fifteen minutes to walk the length of the SouthBank to City Hall. It is a wonderful walk and in the time it takes I see London skyline with St Paul's, Big Ben and Parliament, National Theatre, Royal Festival Hall, The Globe Theatre and even the pretentious Tate Modern, home of elitist Sunday suit wearing bigots. I had a few unpleasant days there and found it trying to preach to me what was good and what was not. They even rack up exhibition prices to see works that often were nothing like as good as the chalk paintings on the pavement by street artists. I would love to give the Turbine Hall over to street artists and have them in each day and create work for the public to watch and also drop a quid in their cap as they work. May be then they would be truly supporting the artist. Sorry Reader, the Tate Modern is open to all, but enjoyed only truly by the select few they want to entertain. The public they just patronise and want your money, but rather you gave them cash and then just left. The Royal Academy however has phenomenal exhibitions and is an amazing space to see art. They really know how to put together an exhibition.

While I have time writing this journal Reader, which is what I am doing whilst sat inside the records room at City Hall, go see anything at the Victoria and Albert Museum. From Bowie to Horst, Constable to McQueen, their curators work with people to put together world breaking shows and events.

I am sat in the records room and have my three zippo lighters next to me on the desk as in walks Tobias. He is surprised to see me and wonders how I got in. He then sees my pink handkerchief and relaxes.

"Feeling bold Sir John?"

"Tobias you tart, how was the weekend?" Now this was actually something I wished I had never asked as Tobias was dying to tell someone about the debauched weekend he had in Brighton with his new boyfriend, Barry, a docker from Plaistow, and how they took back to theirs a complete drag show for a wild party.

I laugh as when I was a young man I used to share a flat and then my house in Wimbledon with a friend. He was gay and I was straight. Every man he bought home fancied me and every woman I managed to pop back for a coffee fancied him. Even his parents came to stay once and when all his camp friends turned up, as they never knew their son was gay, he had made out they were my friends and he spent the night in bed with my girlfriend as I had an evening in Heaven dancing the night away in order to keep up the pretense. Looking back on it I smile. His parents said that they really liked me, but were worried that their son was sharing a flat with a gay man.

One night we were out at Trade, a well-known gay club open from 3am until early morning and I get home with my illustrious flat mate saying he would follow later. I am in bed by 5am and then about an hour later all the lights in the house go on, music up full, party in full swing and my house full of gay men. Not just any gay men, but the whole of the Chippendales Male Strip Troupe. Yes ladies, back in the early nineties most of the incredible male strippers were gay. A couple were not, but from the activity in my house that night I think the straight ones had gone to bed.

I asked Tobias if I was allowed to drink tea in the room and he said that sadly no, but he had a flask downstairs and could bring me a cuppa to sip at the door. I smiled and we hear the door open. It is another sexy looking girl of about twenty-five, graduate and possibly an intern who is on the phone.

"Yes, Quetty, I am in the room now, there are two fellas here with me," she says as she enters.

"Tell Quetty it is Tobias and Sir John."

Tobias looks at me and laughs, "Oh great now everyone will think we were in here shagging."

I have no idea how he made this assumption, but the young girl looks alarmed.

"Don't worry we're just good friends," he says, "anyway I'll go get you something hot." And with this exits.

I look to the vision and can hear Quetty trying to get her attention, but she is in shock from seeing two homosexuals, she is from Leeds. Not a little backwater Reader, a great cosmopolitan city, but areas do have still homophobic inhabitants.

"What's your name?" I ask.

"Doreen."

"Can I have a word with Quetty?"

The girl hands me her mobile. "Hello gorgeous it's me and thanks for saving me from Tobias. Listen if I can help let me know and Doreen and I will do it for you so no one is the wiser as I guess you are still with the PM. Yes I thought so, text us the files and we will deal with from here for you, no worries and tell me more about breakfast with Robert the PM and his wife and you later. Ok text to this phone and will delete once done."

I hand the phone back to Doreen. "OK Quetty, he isn't gay then? Oh good. Laters."

I hear Quetty, "Look after Sir John he is a friend of the PM."

Seems she was from Leeds studied at Goldsmiths and has a hybrid Yorkshire accent with London talk, 'init'.

I sit at the console and suddenly the text comes in with a huge list of files to delete. One says property acquisitions and I note a few other trade files that would be interesting read.

As I am about to start Doreen asks, "Why you got so many zippo lighters, you a heavy smoker?"

I suddenly realise I should of turned them on. I smile, "I am actually trying to think which one to give my new friend as a present, which do you think?"

Doreen leans forward, her large breasts almost falling out of her top and the skirt so tight and short that can see her thong, well what there was of it in the reflection of the computer systems cabinets behind.

"Well I love the one with the skull and crossbones on it."

"Good choice, skull and crossbones it is." I manage to flip the switch on each one and know that as I delete the file will be transferred to my lighters. I had tested them earlier on a file I had on my laptop and still have no idea how it works, just that it does.

We highlight them all and I have Doreen lean over to press delete and she slips her hand onto my crotch as if an accident. "Oh I am so clumsy," she giggles, "don't tell the PM what we get up to will yer?"

As she remains there bending over I slide my hand up between her thighs and stroke her,

"Oops, seems we are both clumsy." She does not flinch, I think this is how this girl could become Minister for the Interior within a few short years, except re-thought that as she swivels on her heels bends over flashing her backside in my face, I think the Minister for the Interior has less than a week to pack.

The door opens and in walks Tobias with his flask.

"Oh put it away Doreen. The man is busy can't you see?"

Doreen rights herself and I take my pen from her hand, I used to do magic tricks as handy as an Invisible.

"Thanks," showing Tobias pen, "gratitude and sorry to say I looked away, but obviously Tobias did not."

"Well I hope you got a picture Tobias, I'll be back, off to powder my nose."

As Doreen exits Tobias calls after her, "Sorry love didn't get a photo as saw highlights coming towards me and dived for cover."

The door slams and I decide to laugh with Tobias. "Wow, that was close. Thanks for that. Great timing, I was a goner there had you not come in."

"I think I would need about twenty stiff ones to come in that." Tobias laughs again at his own jokes.

"So you know Doreen then from..?"

"One of the career girls hired by ex Mayor. All bimbos who truly do lie back and think of the salary, but I feel bad now as we used to be tight. She fell foul of that oaf that used to rule the roost here and ended up a girl that had to do favours to remain here. I got her a job in the agendas section, where we work out strategic plans for what to tackle and how and she was brilliant at it. Then she dumped it all to work directly under the oaf and I lost all respect for her, so ces't la vie as the French say, she has made her bed and looks miserable."

Tobias looked upset, as he really liked Doreen I could see. The door opens and Doreen enters. There is an empty silence as she sits next to me and Tobias looks to leave.

"Tobias, can you sort out a table at the Men's Club for lunch?" Tobias swivels on his heels.

"Of course what time?"

"What time is good for you Doreen?" I ask. Both look at each other. "Come on you two got a lot of catching up to do and a table for three is less conspicuous for idle gossip than two Tobias, don't you think?"

"Why Sir John, I don't know what you mean? Doreen, go on sister name the time,"

"I would be happy anytime."

"We know that love, but for lunch?"

Doreen quips back, "Well how about 1:30 and make sure you order a rubber cushion for yourself as I see you haven't sat down today, big weekend with Barry?"

"I forget how quick you are sister, you better have some good dirt to dish or I will be disappointed." Tobias exits and Doreen smiles at him as he flashes her a smile back.

"So how we doing?"

I look to see only three files deleted and there are over a hundred.

"Tell me about you as we seem to have a while."

Doreen looks to the door.

I continue, "Tobias said and I quote, " 'You got a job in the agendas section, where he works, working out strategic plans for what to tackle and how and you were brilliant at it'."

"He said that? He was so lovely to me and I guess leaving to follow this idiot must have been like disrespectful I guess. But I did it as was put in a position where thought my term was over here anyway. I laugh as I never slept with the asshole, I tossed him off once when we were drunk, but that was all, I never slept with him."

"Your secret is safe with me. Anyway what did you want to do?"

Doreen looked at me as if she was about to tell a naughty secret," Well….. I loved it here and there was a time we had to work out the security and schedule for the Chinese PM guy visiting and so had to visit and coordinate everything for his visit when with the Mayor, as well as organise functions, caterers and entertainment. We hired Shirley Bassey once, my God that woman is a leg-end as she called herself. We really hit it off. Many were scared of her as one guy here screamed 'I love you Shirl.' No one calls her 'Shirl'. She looked really fuming like and about to hurl into a diva fit, but I found myself walking up to her and saying something like, 'don't worry about that twat Miss Bassey, let me get you a mint tea and do you want to come have a sit down in the Mayor's private suite?' She looked at me and I said hi I'm Doreen, nobody special and she took my face in her hands and told me I was and we sat having tea and cucumber sandwiches in the Mayor's private room."

"So what you doing here?" she asked.

I watch as suddenly there are sixty-four files done.

"Me, oh I am nobody also, well next to you I am. I am carrying out a special dossier on the Arts and trying to get this government to fund huge Arts projects across the UK and schools without them realising it. I think you have the ammunition I need also."

"Sorry, what do you mean?"

"I mean Doreen, your story has motivated me to do better and feel you too will see a new opportunity coming your way very soon."

Doreen mistakes this line to be a come on and feeling that a rebuttal may lead to jeopardising my plan I allow myself to succumb to a kiss and a passionate fumble.

Pulling away I mention, "Shame not in the Mayor's Private Rooms as we should have complete privacy and take this further."

"That is not a good idea he films everything, total tool as he told me to work for him and leave here or he'll leak to colleagues my drunken hand job video. He even showed it to me."

"Can I get a copy?" Doreen looked hurt. " As I think we should play a trick on him. May be get other videos and make a fun edit to use for the greater good of Doreen."

"I like you. I like you a lot and yes I reckon the videos must be here somewhere."

"Well look only twenty-three files to download, I mean delete and then lets have a look." I could not believe how men in power feel they are not only above the law, but that they are invincible as they are so clever. Well this idiot was not.

Tobias returns and smiles. "Tables booked and I have a booth for us." He then turns and leaves.

Doreen is excited, "I love the club!"

"Me too. So let's find these video files it seems all on the list is deleted."

I sat there with Doreen laughing at the most bizarre videos of the Mayor dressing up and masturbating as well as having sex with an elderly woman that looked the same age as his mother. Doreen remarked on what a small cock he had and I said that I was not actually looking that much, to which she thought I meant I was eying her up and placed my hand between her thighs. I managed to contain my own excitement, as she was an incredible woman, northern girls are naturally forward I find, and at one point sat astride me and took out her large boobs rubbing them in my face. I enjoyed, but honestly it was a bit funny, I find that sort of sexual activity funny, something for porn films to video, but being suffocated whilst having back of your hair pulled not top of my list. Also I could then not see the screen and asked if we could slow down until we were in the booth alone. This really excited Doreen as she then told me she was a bit of an exhibitionist. Really? I thought!

Just as we managed to compose ourselves and return to the files the door opens and in walks Dougie, Doreen's old boyfriend. As soon as we are introduced and the air seemed like you could cut it with a knife I stood shook his hand and said that I was Sir John and a friend of Tobias's. Dougie immediately relaxed and seemed happy as he thought I was gay.

"You two know each other? I gathered as much. So you are Dougie you say and what do you do here?"

"I work in the Agenda's offices."

"Yes he does. Has my old job." says Doreen upset, "Directly under that slag Phyllis."

"Got it through hard work," Dougie replies.

"Thank God for that!" I exclaimed, "Thought you may of had to take one up the back in the Mayor's private rooms," I retort to which Doreen laughs. Dougie looks embarrassed.

"Did you know he has everything that goes on in that office filmed?"

"What?!" Dougie looks at me alarmed.

I see a file Phyllis's audition tapes.

"It is Ok Dougie we all make mistakes. Been looking at tape of Doreen earlier," Doreen gives me a look of shock," To find her drunk, but still the Mayor couldn't get into her knickers. It really is funny as he waddles around the room after her with his trousers round his ankles. Seems he has anyone meet him there whether they succumb or not he tells a story the way he wants.

226

Listen, we are going to a place close by for lunch would you like to join us?"

Tobias arrives. "My word this place is like Piccadilly Circus and look what the cat dragged in, Dougie."

"I am just leaving."

"One thirty Dougie at the City Hall entrance. Don't be late."

As Dougie leaves he smiles at Doreen and Tobias gives a double take. As the door shuts Tobias looks at Doreen annoyed.

"I remember that a certain boy was awful to a certain girl over a certain untrue rumour not so long ago.."

"And I remember a certain handsome young man being awful to a lovely young girl he should of been a better friend to only moments ago."

Tobias looked crest fallen at me. "I cannot be mad at you. Sorry, Doreen."

"So that's settled then Dougie joining us for lunch at the Club."

Tobias turns with a surprised look on his face.

"Oh come on Tobias, why look surprised it's me here and anyway while they are chatting catching up you can tell me more about Barry and Brighton."

Tobias's face lights up and with a wicked smile he turns and exits laughing. "You kill me Sir John."

When alone we have managed to download all the video files and we close the computer down. It is now 1:15. As I stand to rise Doreen holds my arm.

"But what about us, Sir John?"

I look at this ravishing beauty and wonder why so many beauties huddle around unattractive men in power.

"My darling Doreen, what can I say. You are what? Twenty-five? Ok and Dougie is twenty-four turning twenty-five? Good so the maths has it. I am fifty-four and trust me twenty-four goes into twenty-five more times than fifty-four."

I see Doreen think it through and then gasp as she grasps what I was saying and gives me a hug. "Thank you Sir John."

"Cannot believe I missed out on a hand job," I joke.

"Oh I am sure I sort something out."

"And miss lunch at the club, reigniting with Dougie and getting back in with Tobias, come on girl, we need to get you back here asap."

I collect my zippo lighters and place them in my pocket and see that there is a camera in the computer room.

"One second just need to do one thing."

I quickly find the video file in computer room and show Doreen that deleting last three weeks so no one notices. She smiles and we see delete and computer says that it is recalculating and back on in thirty seconds. We are out of there in ten.

Downstairs we all meet and pass the new Mayor who smiles and we rush to the Men's Club for lunch. I have to be honest that Doreen truly had got my motors started and I looked forward to seeing Megstar later. I then realised I had no real idea what Megstar did. I was thinking of a luxurious bath and... oh yes, Reader you remembered too, I am in Air BnB. Ardour lost.

Well off to The Men's Club and an interesting chat with my new friends and I have somehow managed to secure my mission, well I have dossiers that will lead to the dossier being in one of the ones downloaded, as well as enough ammunition to sink the Bismarck five times over, let alone the Head of the New Order.

I spent the lunch laughing and literally forgetting everything. Who I was, what I was meant to be doing and it was just the tonic, I suggest everyone Reader has a lunch away from everything and just indulges.

Dougie and Doreen were getting on like they had met for the first time and it seems Barry was his man from the Lebanon. I was safe and relaxed and Tobias was paying. What a result, this mission was primed to activate. Wanting to soak in a bath remember Jeremy has showers no bath........

32

I receive a call from Megstar and she has to work late as well as her mother is unwell in Poland. I tell her to rest and that I will see her tomorrow. I would take her to the Commons Bar. Now as I would like to remain invisible it is hard so to be invisible the way forward is to go with the most stunning woman all eyes will be upon and you will soon disappear from view.

I look through the files and remember as I look at one property file that the ex-mayor had been selling off prime land and buildings at knock down prices to his friend and there was a company he sold through owned in his father's name. Seemed he kept it all in the family. Contracts were done through the same firms of architects and builders and they is a file buried where he has meetings with an entrepreneur whose idea he has stolen for his own financial gain to regenerate dark spaces, old underground stations. This is actually one of the more damaging as there is a video recording of the meeting he apparently denies having. In-between all his nefarious sex parties with prostitutes he filmed and they were all short movies. Bit like a Jewish porn movie, one minute of sex and nine minutes of guilt.

I once had a case where I exposed a vitriolic old battle-axe who thought she was related to the Royal family, well her own had disowned her, and how she and her 'business partner' were fleecing their clients as she never told them her silent partner was in fact the builder carrying out loads of work for them, most work never needed to be done, at the properties they managed. I was in there working as an Invisible and the Builder would walk in and

230

have his property manager hat on and get staff member to visit building with him and make a list of maintenance jobs to be done. Back at the office he would instruct the staff member to email his building firm a list of works that they turned up and did without every having second quote, or if there was a second quote it was supplied by another company he owned. Sad to say they still operate, but many that they fleeced moved on and things became harder. I guess in West London talking with a plum in your mouth can fool the smartest of people.

I saw about a hundred files that could bring down the Titanic and started to sit up all night and piece together for my friends the Ministers and another. I deleted the file with my little Doreen. I even watched for a few seconds her and I, then deleted. Oh Reader what could have been?

Then I saw the file that truly scared me and made me realise just how dangerous this new secret order was. It was hidden among all the other files labeled 'Into 10'. My hit, the Head of the New Order was intelligent, but in an evil cunning way, he was not smart intelligent. In it were agreements and funds raised to support his coup to get himself into Number 10 as new leader of party mid-term so no need for public vote. It was cunning and ruthless as I read how they would rebuild the country.

The plans were nothing short of horrific and stirring up racial hatred of immigrants was the key to the plan working. Then I saw that meetings held and agreements signed by four parties. Head of State was one, Head of New Order another and the other two I could not believe. One was the leader of the BNP, who were funding the whole operation, and the other an oily little man, failed to be elected, many times as head of a Get Britain out of Europe Party, and even when promised to resign from that party as leader if lost in last general election showed no integrity and of course did not. This was a nasty piece of work that was happy to openly fuel racial hatred in communities saying that he was just reflecting the mood of the people.

My dear Reader, this was like the black shirts trying to align for power like in the 40's.

I cross-checked video records to find video of them all together and also an horrific one where they had prostitutes and the BNP and failed politician with young boys. It seemed this was a group of men with no integrity, no decency, no boundaries to any debauchery, happy to victimise and harm anyone as long as they got what they wanted. They had this campaign with slogan of 'Make Britain Great Again' and it was nothing more than using power to bully people and everything for their own gain. The New Order was purely for the greater good of themselves.

I found a spread sheet and a list of money paid into accounts off-shore with one sum of £600,000 going into a fund that had no name, but was not off-shore. The plot thickened and I managed to make a separate file that would be handed to a man I thought should have the chance to stop them without major press and harm to the country as often things are subdued or removed without any of us knowing.

Thinking of how things can be removed so easily I saw my reflection in the screen of the laptop and realised I too was in great danger. I had come to realise that with so many exposed this was the situation every Invisible Man has to know is that he has to sacrifice his safety for others. Many had died and disappeared, others on the run like Jimmy, but few ever retire fully, and I knew I had to find another smokescreen to make my aliases real and have them disappear. I then think of Megstar and even sweet young Doreen.

Now Reader, I feel that often it may seem I may of been unfaithful to Megstar here, but it was never as it seems as often you have to go through certain...OK I feel awful as no matter what I should of not allowed it to happen between Doreen and me. Happy to say in the booth she stroked my thigh and Dougie saw to which I quipped that I must be sat the side he normally sat. He then went and looked shocked as if he had just realised he did always sit that side of Doreen and we moved on.

There is a knock on my door and I answer to see Jeremy with a cup of tea. "Saw your light on and thought you might like a cuppa."

I had just finished the files and had shut the computer.

"Thanks just in time. why don't we have this in the kitchen together if you're still up too?"

I saw Jeremy's face light up as I said this and he invited me to the kitchen.

We sat in his lovely flat and started to discuss art and theatre, he had seen John Barr article in his new musical and we had a common bond. I even rang John up and had them talking on Skype. It was just one of those spontaneous moments. John even had two tickets left on

233

the theatre door for Jeremy for Saturday and we laughed and said goodnight to Johnny.

Jeremy looked sad. His partner had died of Aids only three months ago. As he was not married to her the bank want to take up the mortgage and force Jeremy to sell. He is doing Air BnB as he needs to earn the money to afford the house. It was full of momentous and memories of him and his partner. Now Reader I say partner as I want you to come to the wrong conclusion. His partner was a successful city banker and her family hated him and the fact he was an artist. She earns and he painted, but from the photographs and letters they wrote to each other when apart you could see this was two people hopelessly in love.

He had written to his local MP and the name hit a cord with me. The MP wrote back saying nothing he could do, which according to Jeremy is not true. He wanted the MP to write to the bank to see why they did not respond to his claim. Yes there was a dispute with the family wanting ownership, but they had been together for twenty-five years. It seems daft there is anything to contest, but it seems greed in family rules and they blame Jeremy for Lucinda's death. Lucinda and Jeremy met at an exhibition and she was a patron of the arts and he was an artist. It was love at first site and as the family never approved they decided not to marry until the family had changed their views. Lucinda loved her family and it tore her apart and once they never spoke for four years, but it was Jeremy that got everyone back together. After a civil four months they reverted to the vile people they were and Lucinda and Jeremy decided not to let it bother them.

Lucinda contracted the HIV virus through a blood transfusion and had won a huge settlement in court from the NHS. It was nothing more that a mistake by one nurse not screening blood, donated by an elderly woman who also had no idea she was HIV, and so the two placed the money into a fund to decide what to do with at a later date. Well the money sat there for a while and Lucinda became really ill and they forgot about it. It is in their joint account untouched and after she passed they came after her money. The house was in both their names with her half held in trust for reasons he could not remember. It was held by her company she was a shareholder in and her partners in the firm saw it as their asset.

Jeremy had become incredibly sad and I told him that tomorrow night I would take him with a friend of mine for drinks and we will meet his MP face to face.

"You work in the Commons?" he asked.

"No, I am working on something that has given me access and I am bringing my girlfriend so you can be gooseberry."

We both laughed as he enjoyed having someone to talk to as well as someone to talk honestly with. Reader we often skirt around subjects as feel awkward, but often it is easy to talk direct. The trick is to get it out there and move on, NOT get stuck mentioning the elephant in the room every other sentence.

I lay in my bed pondering over the name of his MP and awoke at 5am. Blistering Barnacles, it was a Captain Haddock revelation as I remembered the name. One of the investment bankers mentioned in dodgy dealings with the ex-mayor had the same name. Tonight was going to be a night where I would be visible and vulnerable and then had to magic myself away without anyone remembering where I had appeared from.

Vesna and Ana were safe. Chastity and Henry were safe in Number 10. Tobias was safe as nothing to do with this and Quetty and Robert safe soon I hoped from the previous days meeting. Only Doreen was vulnerable, no not only Doreen, I was going with Megstar to the Commons. I had made a huge error in placing innocent people in the firing line. Tonight was a night I would have to take the bullet. I write this Reader not as a heroic Invisible Man, but a scared individual who fears he will not only lose his freedom, life even, but worse than that the love of his life.

33 I spent the day in the House of Commons. The chambers were full. It was not due to an important debate or that everyone was conscientious, it was everyone was in to sort out their partners and excuses to their wives that they had to work late on Friday as all wanted to be at the Parliamentary Ball. Held in the great hall.

Many were advising their juniors how to dress down as their wives and even husbands were coming as the PM's wife decided after the last years debacle to email all husbands and wives. I must admit I have grown fond of her.

Sat in the bar I have my first meeting. It is with the two ministers and hand them each a zippo lighter download. I kept the lighters myself as not giving these clowns my technology. We have a fabulous lunch and on cue in walks Quentin to join us. It was as brazen as that as armed with their new power they wanted everyone to know they had the power. Quentin was given the Arts file I had prepared. Over six billion pounds of funds to be given out that would only hit the budgets of others slightly. That was their genius and they wanted full credit.

Quentin left with the file full of excitement as this was huge. The enormity of the government doing not a U Turn, but spinning around full circle to change plans made only a year previous by the same two ministers. They were going to be the saviours of the Arts and have demigod status.

I asked for one favour in return, which was dispatched immediately. As my next appointment arrived both Ministers stood and introduced me to Jeremy's MP.

Both said in various words that whatever he does he must make sure their good friend Sir John is not left unhappy. He cowered as if to say of course and this awful little MP sits and tries to smile. He had been summoned and told to do whatever I asked and often it is something all dread.

I open up by ordering a drink. As the waiter serves I smile and we toast.

"So please let me tell you this is going to be painless. It will involve you making two phone calls and then finishing your drink and never mentioning this ever again."

He looks worried and I explain he will call his brother-in-law's firm that have a share in Lucinda's house and firm to relinquish the company rights to her partner Jeremy. Then to call the bank to unlock the instruction on the deeds to the house that should be handed to Jeremy. In return Jeremy will sell his brother Lucinda's shares at full price less a ten percent discount and all matters will cease.

Yes the MP was married to the firm's major shareholder's sister.

At first he pleaded he could not and then I showed him three emails. Each having a dodgy deal with the ex-Mayor giving his brother's firm the contracts on major investments with the City of London. All deals were done once Lucinda had been ill and out of the office.

He was sweating and asked if this was the only time I would ever use this against him? I gave him my word and that tonight I suggest he join us in the bar to meet with Jeremy and hand him the signed deeds. I will then have you lifted to a ministerial role with my two friends who left just now, "I think you know them?" I said with glee.

" What time tonight?"

I looked at him and suggested we make it 7pm. Then we can all enjoy the ball together.

"Thanks for your time and you can go now." I dismissed him and suddenly felt amazing as right on cue walked my next appointment, Henry.

Henry passed the MP and then looked back at me as if to say 'He didn't seem happy'. I smile and stand as if a father greeting his son.

Henry sits and asks what is happening, as he has had to slope off from the Prime Minister's office. "I am allowed a lunch break." Henry says and at that moment the Prime Minister walks in and looks complete agitated. He sees me, as I am holding centre court, I want to be visible. I stand as if the PM has come to see me. He walks over as feels it would be rude not to say hello.

"Prime Minister, I see you are busy, you look like you could do with a drink, but then again keeping your eye on this lot must be a full time job."

He looks at me and apologies. He is now in constituency mode and smiles.

"Prime Minister can I be candid?" I ask.

"Of course, hello Henry is it not?"

Henry stands and shakes the Prime Minister's hand, "Yes Prime Minister, I was just on my lunch.."

"It is OK Henry," I interject, "we are all among friends. Prime Minister I gather you have just seen the leaked dossier on the Arts that I have been helping promote."

"You..you! This is your handiwork is it?" He is trying to hide his anger.

"Yes and also a band loyal to you."

"What!"

I call to the waiter, "Can we get some water and a couple of sandwiches for the Prime Minister and my friend here."

"I haven't got time for this!" he says under his breath.

" I'm sorry Prime Minister.." starts Henry.

"Henry is sorry we did this without consulting you first, but these walls talk and there is a New Order in town."

The PM sits and looks daggers at me.

"Listen, I have to be honest I never voted for you, but wondered why you did so many damaging things with austerity and thought there must be a file on you. Well I found the file and the photo is damaging, but slightly photoshopped. I also have this file compiled by my young friends of democracy they call themselves.

"What?" and even Henry exclaims "What?"

"I have the complete list of the New Order and the name of the Head. I have damaging material that could see them locked up in prison for years, sadly that would indict you as well and it seems you have been helpless to stop."

"You have the names as well as the evidence, and all the evidence that the Head of the New Order has on those in the Order."

"How can I believe you?" asks the PM.

"Ah sandwiches, a wonderful selection, thank you. So let me say this, I have film of your Chancellor in a gimp suit with the Israeli PM's son."

"What?"

"He is careless and the files for this have all been deleted. The Head has a condemning show reel of his antics and illegal activities not only in files, but on video connecting him to every dodgy deal done selling off London assets to friends. Actually that is all his members of the Order have. They do not have the dirt I have that he had on them and through his own stupidity he has had erased yesterday morning. Prime Minister here is the files on this drive. Put together by a crack team of activists that were fed up with the corruption inside these walls and tying your hands from doing the right thing."

"I think I need a drink. Waiter can I get a lemonade?" He looks at Henry, "and a Gin and Tonic for my friend here Henry. What you drinking Sir John, shall I continue to call you Sir John?"

"I am fine with my coca cola Prime Minister."

"Phillip, I need you to cancel my next meeting back fifteen minutes I am having a sandwich, I think I deserve a sandwich. Actually, who am I meeting?"

"The Leader of the Opposition Prime Minister," says Phillip.

"Then have him join us Prime Minister so we can all enjoy these amazing sandwiches."

The PM takes one look at me as if a weight has been lifted off his shoulders. "Yes tell the old fart, sorry, right honourable gentleman lets have tea in the bar. Enough behind closed doors crap I think."

"Yes Prime Minister," and Phillip exits.

"What Henry and I suggest is you read just the dossier on these two." I hand files showing both the Minister for Health and Secretary for State. Both have decided to leak this document and take full credit and want to move themselves into the role of over seeing the huge revenues they have maneuvered. Truth is from these two documents you can see one minister is a director and silent majority holder in his sister's theatre group where he plans to invest hundreds of millions via an off-shore tax account, no offence intended (as PM embroiled in his own scandal) but this one also has just opened up a

242

touring theatre group that will also benefit millions of pounds from link to a similar off-shore account."

"This is fabulous, but it damages everything, me and.. is this a blackmail, you blackmailing the Prime Minister of Great Britain?"

"No Prime Minister we are giving you the fuel to take credit for the Arts scheme, cut off the chains that bind you in office from doing what you set out to do and free reign to make things better. All I ask is you reward your close allies."

"That'll be you would it Sir John?"

"No Prime Minister, after tonight I will be no longer visible. A myth or a moth if you have a lisp." The Prime Minister and Henry look confused.

"This dossier is the work of Henry and Chastity, who you met with your wife the other night and a young girl who placed her life on the line to get this for you with her boyfriend, a list here. I feel you need good people around you, Henry and Chastity are the brightest couple in their internment year and both want to do more so use them. Doreen and Dougie want to be running the Mayor's Agenda Office with emphasis on Security that is where I feel Henry and Chastity best placed with your security and events, I then feel the post of intermediary between the Mayor of London and the Prime Minister's office be set up and given to another of the group Tobias Ruffalo, at least he won't be caught trying to compromise young ladies. Try to have someone close watch the ex-Mayor with his trousers down as not a pretty sight. Oh and two of our group were given new identities after the shoot out on the Square.."

"That was you?!" asks Henry.

"No, but there were serious connections and they had to be sadly lifted to safety, but saw this lovely hotel that needs to be run and as a present I feel it would suffice from the witness protection funds. It has yet to be signed and sealed."

"This seems to be a pretty comprehensive list and files Sir John, what is your real name?" asked the Prime Minister.

"Well he has been Dudley Ramsden as well," says Henry.

"So you have no idea either then?" The PM says to Henry. " Good let's keep it that way."

"One last thing, you will be announcing the Arts Funding and also a cabinet reshuffle is due I think, but the latter is all down to you. I just want you to have a clean slate. Take the credit as this Arts budget will not hurt the economy and lift the countries spirits as plays, theatres, cinema and music all get a lift and a nation enjoying Shakespeare in his 400th year together realising we all must experience escapism and be entertained in troubled times as we all fight together to regain the stability of our country."

"I wish I had said that."

"Oh you may Prime Minister it is all in the speech outline, but here comes the leader for the opposition." I stand to shake his hand and he seems confused.

"Sit down Gerald, I have a cunning plan and want your thoughts on it." The PM beamed and turned to Henry. Opening the file and looking at list he looked to Henry,

"Henry can you, sorry, Gerald this is Sir John who helped the new Arts budget and Henry part of a new team organising agendas and making sure we engage through the Arts with our voters. Henry have all these four in my offices at 4:30pm today without fail as need to have a chat."

"Yes Prime Minister," says Henry beaming with pride and looks at me as I wink and tell him to go.

"I thought you were going to kill the Arts like all Tories," say the Leader for the Opposition.

"Gentlemen, I feel I should leave you both and I will have more cucumber sandwiches sent over they are really lovely. You're a vegetarian are you not sir?"

The Leader of the Opposition looks and smiles, "Yes I am, well the wife wanted to be and I love her so much, plus you don't want to argue with her.."

"You see gentlemen you have so much in common, great taste in women. I bid you farewell and will be having drinks later as one last thing to do before I go."

The Prime Minister stands and shakes my hand, " Sir John thank you and I think I will look into the Venetian situation immediately."

I shake both their hands and as I exit I hear the PM say, "You know he voted for you."

"Seems like a clever man," came the reply as a plate of cucumber sandwiches passes me on the way out.

34

Back at Jeremy's I hear him shouting from the lounge to me upstairs. " Sir John Sir John you'll never believe what has just happened... come quick!"

I walk into the lounge and there is the Prime Minister announcing the new Arts budget. Next to him is the Leader for the Opposition and both looked relaxed and joking saying,

"That it is great to make this country, the greatest country for the Arts, once more a haven for artists. This Arts budget will not hurt the economy and lift the countries spirits as plays, theatres, cinema and music all get a lift and a nation enjoying Shakespeare in his 400th year together realising we all must experience escapism and be entertained in troubled times as we all fight together to regain the stability of our country. My learned friend and colleague may not always see eye to eye with me, but together we stand united on this. Plus both our wives, true Arts lovers are happy with both of us and we want the nation to share in our joy."

"It is amazing. If only Lucinda could of witnessed that."

"My friend there is another surprise I have for you tonight so get you jacket and let us pick up Megstar and make our way by taxi, and all on me tonight, well the government as have their credit card, so please come and live your life and celebrate your wife's memory as I feel I know she would of wanted you to."

It is in the back of the car I look at Jeremy, the worry and stress he has been under has taken its toll.

247

"You know what? I cannot believe how inspired I have been by that on the telly. Politicians finally understanding what life is truly about. We are a nation of people not numbers; sure they have to balance the books, but remember that the human heart will support better if happy than sad." And with that said I watched Jeremy as he looked out the taxi window with a tear in his eye.

We collect Megstar and she looks amazing. I am filled with pride.

"You look wonderful, my name is..."

"Jeremy, I know. It is an pleasure to meet you and thanks for letting me share this evening with you."

Megstar was just magnificent and laughed," At last decent male company, you are an artist are you not. I recently went to the Royal Academy and saw work by a new artist called 'My Love' it was so moving. Did you see it?"

Jeremy smiled and a tear hit his eye, "It was my last painting of my beautiful Lucinda."

Who would of thought that Jeremy was such a renowned artist and also lost his drive due to corrupt officials. We arrive at the Commons and as we enter people nod and smile at me. In a corner chatting are the wives of the Leader of the Opposition and the Prime Minister. Jeremy please we need to meet someone quickly. I lead Megstar over with Jeremy to the ladies and introduce them all. I order drinks and then make excuses for Jeremy and I.

At the bar I speak to the man behind Jeremy, "Jeremy, I believe you have not met, but this is your MP and well well well, the partner in your wife's business."

Jeremy turns and looks confused and from behind him I nod for them to explain.

"Hello Jeremy, huge apologies for the cock ups and I had no idea as to what was going on all a huge misunderstanding. So we wanted to hand to you in person the deeds to the house and mortgage is paid off as per Lucinda's wishes and if we may be presumptuous like to buy your shares in the company for asking price less ten percent."

Jeremy is stunned and looks to me as if to say what is happening.

"I am sure that would be acceptable and the compensation money left to Lucinda I think you should make a foundation in Lucinda's name," I said. "Now in light of the Prime Minister's new Art initiative I thought that the centre Lucinda was treated in for HIV as well as other centres we can fund galleries where art classes can be held as well as exhibitions of their work hung. What do you say Jeremy?"

Still dumbstruck Jeremy starts to cry, "Lucinda would love that."

" Not only that I think we should take this opportunity to discuss this with the PM and make their wives patrons. Be phenomenal good business for the firm, good for careers and Jeremy would be painter in residence. What do you say gentlemen?"

Both seem delighted and I say, " OK folks follow me." We walk over to the ladies and I introduce everyone.

"You were the artist for ' My Love ' at the Royal Academy?" asked the Leader for the Oppositions wife, " Megstar told us and it seems we both saw it."

"I was so moved. You captured your wives last moments with …." Said the PM's wife and both are in tears.

"Ladies, may I tell you that Jeremy is to paint again as a new artist in residence in a series of galleries funded for by his late wife's fund at all the major HIV centres in London."

"I cannot believe this day can get any better," says the wife of the Leader of the Opposition.

With the commotion both opposite leaders rush to their wives. The PM looks at me as if to say 'more revelations?'

"Darling, this is the artist behind the painting My Love we both adored," said the Leader of the opposition's wife.

"And he and these wonderful men are helping fund galleries at major HIV centres where he will be giving lessons as artist in residence." The PM's wife hugs her husband's arm.

"Hello, I am the Prime Minister.."

"I know who you are sir, and today's announcement is the single most amazing thing any one Prime Minister has done for the people that has ever been done," Jeremy says and then shakes the PM's hand.

I whisper in the Leader for the Oppositions ear and he steps forward, "Gentlemen this is a wonderful gift and the painting truly moved the wife and I and if I may be so bold I was wondering would you accept me forwarding mine, and the Prime Minister's wife as patrons?"

I can see their joy as Jeremy and all cannot believe how they all benefit. For a moment there is a silence in the bar as all watch this strange band of people, who hold great offices, but are still just people at heart, crying and hugging each other. In true statesman manner the Prime Minister holds aloft his hands and all goes quiet.

"What a day this has been. I stand here proudly, shoulder to shoulder with my esteemed colleague and our wonderful wives to come together for the Arts. Now many worry about the size of the budget and how we can do more elsewhere, but tonight our loved ones and this wonderful painter with his MP and the firm of his wife, create unity through the Arts. We are a people, who breath live and die. All the same, the same blood flows through our veins and tonight we rejoice that we have collectively made the country a better, happily place for all. And tomorrow we stand opposite each other on the commons floor all fighting for what we want, but remembering we are here by the grace of the people."

"Prime Minister, if I may?" interjects the Leader for the Opposition, "blimey this is hard agreeing with a Tory," all cheer and he raises his hands to calm them, "I would like us all to charge our glasses and raise a toast, in fact I see the speaker of the house who recently made a nice sum from a celebrity TV show he was on, so I think Mr. Speaker if you would like to buy a round for all assembled," again all cheer and I see the PM nod at him, and then waiters who know what everyone drinks rush round with drinks. "Prime Minister, you have today done a noble thing. You have proved yourself, I hope no one is filming this for YouTube, you have proved yourself as worthy on this one issue of the office you hold. So with drinks in hand, we all have a drink, hand on, hang on, hang on, Mr. Speaker, a scotch for me and the Prime Minister," again all cheer and laugh, "ladies and gentlemen, we are privileged to be here and now we all have a drink in hand I would like to give a toast, To the Prime Minister of Great Britain and the to the People that we should never forget we serve."

Huge cheers are raised and the atmosphere is electric as all hug each other and I notice the Ministers for State and Minister for Health absent. The PM sees me look round.

"Sir John, seems I owe you.."

"Nothing Prime Minister except be true to your heart, be true to the people and remember an Invisible Army of People will always be watching."

"Your two chums have decided to take the night off and will be returning to office in the morning for us to work out ways forward. I am not sacking them as best keep them where I can see them, don't you think?"

I smile at the Prime Minister and he talks to Jeremy and his wife. Megstar slips away and gives me a kiss. I look around and all are interacting and as I watch the PM slip out with the Leader of the Opposition later I reflect on what was achieved. Did I achieve my mission as the man I did not vote for made into a God and then I reflect.

I see so many happy faces and actually, OK, it is true I did find the dossier and also unearthed a New Order and crushed as career politicians looking to run country for themselves; ended up with politicians realising running country for people.

I see Chastity and Henry equals together, Quetty and Robert laughing together and looks like another partnership growing stronger, despots derailed, country gets new lease of life, and Vesna and Ana running a small boutique hotel in Venice. I had no idea anything would turn out like this and yet more than this I fell in love. Megstar is just breath taking, amazing and words truly cannot describe.

I think of Tobias and Barry travelling the world sorting out all major events and agendas for the Mayor who ever they are as an ambassador between Mayor's office and Number 10. Doreen and Dougie, I smile as see their initials as DD, double D's, and that was Doreen, but they too have dream jobs and an in to an inner circle. I hope that all the youngsters do not become jaded and work there way up to manage the country with passion and heart, understanding that we are a people and helping more Invisibles like me hang up our boots.

I wake at Megastars and as I am in the bath a tired naked Chastity enters and sits on the toilet. She doesn't even see me, I am invisible and I smile to myself.

Megstar receives a call that her mother is unwell in Poland and I drive her to the airport and I am standing here alone. Tonight is the Parliamentary Ball and I have no partner and no reason to go. I think it will be fine and best I make my way somewhere to rest up.

35

I am back in Exeter and having a coffee at the Boston Tea Party. Emma grins at me as if to say hello stranger. It feels always good to come back to familiar places. Beth rushes past and tells me she has been in Honition branch and Elliot passes with two coffees.

Leon is there beautifully sculpted beard and waxed moustache gives me a hearty welcome and I ask after Sophie who is performing tonight in Lynton and Lynmouth. As I exit I see the lovely Mandy now working elsewhere and it seems here is a city that is friendly like a town feels. I see Beth as I sit come with my poached eggs on toast, tall stunning young lady who offered me a free coffee at the Boston to get me in and they all then got me hooked. Even Elliot gives me another smile and a welcome back as he hands me my latte.

I have a wonderful lunch at Lloyd's Kitchen. Emma, a vicar's daughter is just sublime. The service is exceptional and helped by Coral, who says she is called Coral as in Nemo's mum. I love the reference and these two stunning young girls entertain and make me feel welcome. I wish more places would make us all feel welcome.

I sit and see a Big Issue Seller outside and ask if I can move to the table outside and they say fine. I ask him to join me, his name is Joe and a really lovely guy. The staff bring menus and treat us both the same. Joe at first feels he can only order so much and I tell him that today he eats whatever he wants as I intend to.

It is as Joe and I sit and chat and drink copious bottles of water. Emma and Coral are delightful and Joe thinks it is the best day he has had in ages. I had to agree I did too.

Sitting with Joe, he tells me of his plans to start his own paper, a local paper with local news, and still help homeless and get people on their feet. He tells me of the University people and locals all support and how he just needs a printer to help bring the costs down. He was inspirational and I smile as the Big Issue Seller I saw at the beginning of this journal.

As we chatted and sit in the sunshine I think of Megstar and about everything I have written in this journal.

Both Joe and I are full to the brim we sit back, say nothing and watch the people pass us by. But both laugh as they see him, a Big Issue Seller sat in a restaurant enjoying the day, he is visible.

My new friend, Reader, I truly hope you have enjoyed and if you feel like becoming an invisible please note my final thoughts.

You do not have to be visible to do the right thing, you do not have to be visible to do a good deed. You just have to know that we all can make a difference.

Often the joy is to see someone happy and know you contributed. That is enough and those that care they will see the Invisibles around; they will know what you have done.

So look deeper than the facade, past the promises and see the truth, often behind the lie. Make your voice heard.

Much of what has happened and recorded in this journal has happened by reacting to circumstances, but always in a positive way. Seeing those around you and complimenting them, suddenly doors open, trust is given as you are not there trying to get something for yourself. My thoughts are broken by my mobile.

I answer as it is a number nobody has. It is Jimmy.

"Hello Jimmy?"

"Listen I heard you were settling down with Polish girl, but there is trouble in Venice."

The phone dies and I think Vesna and Ana.

I call Megstar and she does not answer. I call the airport for flights to Venice and book a flight for tomorrow.

Joe watches me and smiles, "Busy life eh fella?"

"Yes, sort of."

Joe looks at me and keeps smiling, "Thanks for this, I felt human again. Emma and Coral return to the table to see if we want anything else and I ask for the bill.

"Excuse me?" says Emma to Joe. "I hope you do not mind, but the boss was asking after you and wondered if you fancy a job in the kitchen?"

Joe looks at me and then to Emma, "Yes, years ago I was a chef." Joe looks to me, "You are a lucky charm my friend." I smile as if by thought process Lloyd's Kitchen had shown by a small gesture they have changed a life.

I pay and thank the girls. I walk to my little car and start to pack a bag I am off to Venice. I wonder if Megstar can come for the ride.

I ride on the bus to the airport. Jimmy had worried me, but I sat on the bus and walked through the security without a person noticing me there. I was invisible again.